# TERESA M. ASH

# RESCUE IN TIME

ISBN
978-1-961601-68-0 (Paperback)
978-1-961601-69-7 (eBook)

# RESCUE IN TIME

# TABLE OF CONTENTS

# THEME

The Interplanetary Council of diplomats has chosen earth as their next planet to explore and hope to form diplomatic relations. The Council hopes to find a planet where goodness thrives since they live, move, and breathe in it just as humans nourish themselves with food and water. The Counsel intends to send their best representatives to scout the planet and determine whether the humans are worthy of saving or not. Meanwhile, another faction of aliens intends to destroy all of the earth's inhabitants and use the resources for personal gain. The last thing they want is for the Council to gain strength through consuming the goodness of the inhabitants of another planet.

# INTRODUCTION

The leading character, Tom Clancey, thought his grandfather was simply a senile old man living out his last days in some sort of fantasy until, on his 21th birthday, his grandfather revealed a secret hidden in his most treasured possession, an antique clock. Tom is stunned when the clock reveals that his grandfather is the only living soul on earth entrusted to be the point of contact and the ambassador to visitors from distant worlds. He is equally amazed to discover that the mantle has been passed down to him.

Now at 28, and on his own, equipping these visitors to adapt to earth in his one bedroom apartment is a major challenge. However, the amazing adventures begin when the 12 inch, doll-like visitor, known as G. W. Carver, is unwittingly stolen by a thief. The adventures continue when the dragon-like visitor is swept away by the Colorado rapids. Terry, his wife finds herself being swept away as well, but soon recovers and makes her way to land. And, one of the greatest challenges for this team of visitors is in trying to meet the demands of Cally, the sexy shape-shifter.

Their quest is to save the world from dastardly warlords in the heavens who believe they can put this planet, known as earth, to better use.

# PRELUDE

They represent a total of 9 planets located in three universes spread throughout the Nubian Sea Galaxy. However, only 3 species are to be selected to actually make first contact with the most primitive species known to them all as *humans*.

The interplanetary Council members consist of the following:

The Tarians are olive green, khaki tan, and yellow striped. They slither on their bellies like cobras reared back for an attack and are the size of full-grown 6 foot tall human beings.

The Nubians have long giraffe-like necks and colorful male peacock feathered tails. But unlike most creatures, below the waist they only have two long lanky legs and no visible waistline.

The Mawtojwas (má-tá-was) are in pure crystal blue liquid form and have to stay in liquid stasis most of the time in order to avoid contamination. The liquid, which is clearly visible to the naked eye, flows in and out of itself like the flow of a river and constantly emanates low pulses of ocean blue light.

The Crustacous are small elf-like creatures that always wear hooded woolen brown monk-like capes in order to keep their fragile bodies warm. They stay in heated chambers far too hot for any of the other species to survive for any length of time and they have very pale thin skin, extremely sensitive to light of any kind. And also, their blood can clearly be seen pulsating through their pencil thin veins.

The Junipahs are neither plant nor mammal, male nor female, but are creatures of brilliant rainbow shimmering lights. They are held in continual stasis as well and they are much too bright for the natural eye to gaze upon, therefore, they encase themselves in gold metallic suits at all times.

The Lopus is one of the life forms selected to be ambassador to earth by the Council. The Lopus reside somewhere within the Nubian Sea Galaxy, however, no one knows exactly where. It was chosen because of its' ability to take on any form it chooses; its' kinetic abilities; and its' multi-linguistic talents. It is capable of being understood in more than a thousand languages simultaneously. No one, apart from their sire, really knows their true identity and on this occasion it will assume a human female form.

The Lizaradactiles have been selected to accompany the Lopus on the journey to earth. These creatures, from the planet Prehisteria, have bodies that closely resemble dragons. They can withstand the full force of any human hand held projectile weapon and can destroy any human being by crushing them with only one hand. They also are superb hunters and are known for their keen tracking instincts. The Council unanimously agrees they will make the best bodyguards and since they are the height and size of the average human being, they can easily be camouflaged.

The Rumerangues, who mostly reside on Aquarian, insisted that their representative be allowed to visit earth along with the other ambassadors. They reasoned that because of their information gathering technology they can provide valuable assistance. The problem the Council members have with this species is that they are only the height of a pencil and the width of a Barbie doll. They, for the most part, possess the appearance of a human. Their flattened foreheads, shaped by alligator-type ridges in the center, are hardly even noticeable. Nevertheless, in order to have their demands met, the Rumerangue had to agree to surgically alter it's forehead to resemble that of a human's. He is expected to assume the role of a human doll unless otherwise needed.

The Interplanetary Council of aliens meet on Venus at least once every full planet rotation to discuss improving their sectors. This meeting, however, is about sending a group of scouts to earth in order to save it from total annihilation.

# BOOK 1

# CHAPTER 1

# VISITORS ARRIVAL

It would suffice to say that cherub wings are totally out of the question. This was and still is the debate among the four celestial visitors sent to gather information about Earth.

"We were not sent to this planet to prance around like mythical creatures," says the Lopus and leader of the group.

"We are well aware of the traditional perception of angels on this planet," says the Rumerangue. "However, I for one would've liked being change into a majestic celestial being with wings."

"That simply is not practical thinking," says the Lopus.

"That's easy for you to say with your shape-shifting abilities. You can look like anyone you wish at a moment's notice," says the Rumerangue.

"Is this true? Can you really assume any form?" asks the female Lizaradactile. "Why did you get that kind of power?" Her Lizaradactile partner stares over her shoulder at the Lopus.

"We all have something valuable to offer on this mission," she says. "The Rumerangue is small as a pen in statue. He'll be able to infiltrate places the rest of us can't." He climbs on top of her shoulder to face the others. "Now you two Lizaradactiles have strength and hunter instincts coveted throughout the galaxy," she tells them. "You all should be proud."

Their mode of transportation to earth from the other side of the galaxy was anything but easy. They were given strict orders from the Council of Celestial Elders, to avoid using their wings and powers. They made arrangements for them to hitch a ride on the Synergy of light floating around the universe. The Council had them all reduced down to microscopic particles. They were placed inside a tube-like vessel. Then, they were transported to earth on several beams of light.

As soon as the four of them reached Earth, these high energy particles accumulated over a field. They hovered, then, rapidly swirled around and formed four equal masses. The particles suddenly became gas. The gas vibrated into liquid. The liquid separated into fourths. The separate sections solidified into four figures. One figure assumed the shape of a well-sculptured woman. Another figure materialized into a figurine the height and width of a 12-inch nutcracker. The last two aliens came into view with skin as dense as that of an armadillo and stand as upright as a human.

The Lopus was instructed simply to observe and casually intermingle with as many humans as possible. The Lizaradactiles were instructed to do the same. However, the Rumerangue was sent to observe his colleagues and to record their every move. He needs to make sure they never find out his true mission. He is in league with the most scrupulous characters of the known universe. They simply refer to themselves as the Outcasts. They promise the Rumerangue something more precious than gold. They promise him mortality. On the other hand, the Council demanded he change his physical appearance. For him to become a part of this expedition to earth, he had to comply with their wishes. He plays the game that has been allotted to him even though he does not believe the Council knows what is best for him or the humans.

He survived persecution and war on his planet called Aquarian. He was the only survivor of his clan who was ostracized for being living cybernetics. The thought of living another millennium alone is too much to stomach. This is his chance to finally die. All he has to do is give a bad report about the humans and his colleagues. Then, the Outcasts will be free to destroy another planet. They thrive on destruction and death.

# CHAPTER 2

# HUMAN ENCOUNTERS

A pack of coyotes find pleasure in howling at the moon until intruders enter their domain. The Rumerangue is noticeably bothered by the noise.

"Someone needs to quiet those beasts!" he says. He takes refuge in the backpack slung over the shoulders of the Lopus. Stuffing pieces of tissue in his ears adequately muffle the barking.

"They're not beasts. They're dogs," the Lopus emphatically corrects. "And they're more afraid of you than you are of them."

He hears her loud and clear even though the tissue is still plugging both ears.

"What's the difference," he shrugs. "They're still annoying and frightening creatures."

She widens her stride and with the wave of a hand encourages the others to keep up the hurried pace.

She wants to reach their designated contact before dawn.

"Who says I'm afraid?" defends the Rumerangue.

"No one is saying you're afraid," she sighs. "That was simply an observation." The last thing she wants is to start an argument with the Rumerangue. They are known for arguing their point to the death.

The Lopus remains silent while considering taking control of the noisome animals by projecting fear into their psyches. No, she tells herself, using my abilities now is not logical or fruit-bearing in the long-run. She reminds herself to stay focused primarily on the mission. Their mission is to search for notable redeemable qualities among the inhabitants of this world. If they find the qualities the Council seeks, then, the earth will be spared. Without these redeemable qualities in place, certain interplanetary

Council members will perish. The goodness of others emits an electrical charge into the atmosphere, and they live, move, and breathe in the same way humans nourish themselves with food. She hopes there is goodness on this planet.

The Lopus did not join this mission under her own volition. The Council handpicked the Lopus for this mission, then, they sent her to school to learn the importance of it all. Another part of her mandate is to convey the importance of their mission to the rest of the team. So far, she notices that the Lizaradactiles, who are covered with armadillo-like skin, are treating their visit to earth like a fieldtrip. She may need to use stronger tactics to get them to understand the severity of their mission.

The male Lizaradactile sniffs the air as he bulldozes his way through tall golden grass. His mate follows close behind and knows to stand clear of any foliage bound to pop back into her face. The Lopus is not so lucky. She spits out the grass and gags on the bugs that just caught her by surprise. She won't let that happen again, so, she darts around them and makes her way to the front of the line.

The male Lizaradactile is becoming annoyed by the excessive barking of the coyotes.

"They're still barking," he complains. His feet scrape the heel of the Lopus.

She hops on one foot to readjust her shoe. "Don't worry about it," she tells him. She silences them with thought. They listen to her and obey.

It suddenly occurs to her that they all have yet to choose human names. Hundreds of names race through her memory until one stands out more than the rest.

"I've got it!" she shouts while coming to an abrupt stop. The Lizaradactiles plummet head over heels on top of her. She's pinned to the ground. "Get off of me you beasts!"

The Rumerangue topples headfirst out of the backpack. "Watch where you're going you blundering fools!"

She stands to her feet. "Names. Everybody think names," she says.

"What does everyone think about the name Cally?" she pauses. "Cally Farms!" There is no drum roll of acceptance, even though she would like to have had one. "Get it?" she chuckles. "Farm will help us to remember that we parked our ship way out here near these farms."

"What ship?" the Rumerangue wonders. "We did not come in a ship. We hitched a ride on a beam of light."

The male Lizaradactile helps his mate to her feet. "Thank you, sweetie," she says. His huffing and puffing have her concerned. "It looks like you're the one who can use some help." She straightens her shifted cape and cuts an eye at the Lopus. A brisk wind lifts the capes high over their heads. These capes are especially designed to conceal the Lizaradactiles' large heads and box-shaped frames. Their appearance, according to human standards, is menacing and certainly not for the faint at heart. The female Lizaradactile fights against the next gust of wind by looping her cape over one shoulder. Then, after much a-do, she manages to secure it with the accompanying ties and does the same for her mate. After wrestling with the wind, they are still expected to come up with their names.

"That's it!" the female Lizaradactile. "Frank is a perfect name for you sweetie!"

She has decided to call herself Terry.

"I can get used to Terry," he tells her. "Hey…I think I'll call you Terry…even after we go back home."

Terry is pleased with herself for remembering these names. She read about them in a textbook about earth.

"These names are so cute; don't you agree Frank dear?" Terry giggles in her usual girly shrill.

Frank is nonchalant about the matter and doesn't bother to respond. His only concern is in finding something to eat along the way.

A nearby hoot catches his attention. His eyes dart in pursuit of the bird. With the stealth of a fox, he chases after the Great Horned Owl. "Awe…" he growls while successfully pinning the bird down and holding it between two strong knees. He uses his sturdy hands to rip off the head for Terry. Then, he devours the remaining body in a few swift bites. The horned owl is the largest owl in North America and stands as tall as two feet. This kill certainly will serve as a hearty treat for him. Even so, Frank and Terry are far from satisfied. They're going to need more food very soon.

The Rumerangue, now powered down in Cally's backpack, has chosen a name as well. After studying human history, he selects the name George Washington Carver. He admires G. W. Carver, an African American agricultural scientist and inventor. He was known as the "Peanut Man" because of the hundreds of ways he used peanuts. Most of all, he cared more about people than money. The Rumerangue wishes he could be like Carver. He especially admires Carver for being a leader and excellent role model for his people. The African Americans were oppressed and discriminated against like his peers were on Aquarian. He likes Carver because he shined in the face of adversity.

While being propped high on Cally's shoulder, lights of the city ahead come into view.

"Denver is more primitive than I thought," Frank notices while licking the bloody remains of his prey off his fingers. "Where are all the people?"

"Maybe we'll run across more people over the hill up ahead. The lights are shining the brightest over there," Cally guesses. She can tell that her keen senses are not as sharp as they should be. She mentally calculates the distance from where they're standing to the lights. "Hum…Thirty minutes away," she eagerly announces, but quickly frowns the moment she realizes their human liaison is located approximately 60 miles north of their current location. "All aboard for Denver 60 miles north," she thinks. She conceals her disappointment with a smile and pushes towards the lights. "I don't know what is affecting my senses," she says. "No worries. I'll get us back on track." But first, she wants to find a place to eat and drink sustenance before venturing out on foot again.

# HIDDEN POWERS UNVEILED

UNVEILED

Thirty long minutes pass before the group strolls into the sparsely populated town of Colorado Springs. Tired, yet eager to make first contact, the group follows the enticing aromas coming from the coffee shop up ahead.

"Now we can find out whether these humans are worth saving or not," Frank says through a drawn-out yawn.

He rambunctiously leaps ahead of the group to explore the inside of the coffee shop. The enticing aromas have him drooling all over his shirt. Like a dog on a leash, he is led into the quaint shop.

Once inside, he notices a middle-aged couple seated in a booth nearest to the door. The man curiously looks up at him and scoffs at Frank's appearance. He assumes Frank is dressed for a costume party. while the woman's head remains buried in a book. The woman takes a sip of her coffee before looking up at Frank. "Whew!" she says. "You're dressed for the part…Aren't you?" Frank smiles, then, snuggles the hood around his head. Another man seated at a corner booth raises an eyebrow at him and tugs on the bib of his black cap. Frank seats himself on an orange vinyl bar stool, then, clears his throat at the server. She is busy wiping counters tops and offering refills.

Outside, the rest of the group huddles around Cally for a meeting. "I just want to make it perfectly clear that while on planet earth, we are humans. We are to behave ourselves like humans at all times and we all need to follow my lead at all times," she explains.

Terry fidgets while raising a hand for Cally to acknowledge.

"We still have 60 miles to go, and I don't want anyone to worry…I'm here for you," she says before recognizing Terry's hand. "Yes…What is it?"

"I was just wondering if you know where Frank ran off to."

"Frank…Don't you know?" Cally's calm fades into panic. "I thought he was with you."

Terry twirls around. "Nope…Not here!"

G. W. Carver clears his throat while perched on Cally's shoulder. "Well, I tried to tell you before I was rudely shutdown," he gripes. "Look inside that diner over there," he points across the road.

Cally hopes to sneak up on Frank and give him the tongue lashing he deserves. However, the moment she walks through the doorway of the diner, the door snaps shut behind her and triggers the bell to jingle above it. She ducks and halfway expects something to drop down on her.

Frank glances back at the door which causes his hood to fall over his broad shoulders.

"Oh!" gasps Cally while flinging the hood over his head and exchanging nervous glances with the server. The puzzled server gulps a smile.

"What can I do for you? Are you two together?" She quickly wipes the already-clean counter. "Can I bring you a cup of coffee…Water…Ah…," she pauses. "Food?"

Frank has already eaten two ham sandwiches, one whole apple pie and a large bowl of chili. "Yes!" he nods with a grin.

Cally says a firm, "No!"

"Food…Coffee…Yes!" Frank demands while banging a heavy fist down onto the counter.

As far as he is concerned, doing without food is not an option. The frightened server slips into the back room to call the police. She promptly returns, carrying a cup of coffee and roast beef sandwich. Trembling hands sit both items down in front of Frank.

"Sorry Miss," Cally apologizes.

The fiery spark in Frank's eyes reminds the server of a dragon. You know, the mythical, fire breathing creature often found in storybooks. She wonders whether Frank is dressed in a costume or is truly a creature from another world. She shutters at the thought while being anxious for the police to arrive.

"Outside Frank," Cally sternly orders and points towards the door. "I won't tell you again." Her voice deepens with authority.

The stern looks on her face and the anger in her eyes startles him. He could swear, if only for a moment, her eyes lit up like fire. There is no more resistance in his walk. He allows her to guide him to the door like a lost pup.

"Sorry…It won't happen again," Cally apologizes while glancing back at the server.

"Wait a minute! Who is going to pay for his food?" the server yells.

Cally pushes Frank to the door. "I'll send you the money, unless you're willing to take a bar of gold."

"What?" the server frowns. "We only take cash money here."

The Interplanetary Council forewarned Cally about the Lizaradactiles stubbornness. Cally was so certain she would be able to manage every situation with ease. However, here we are, she thinks, and already I am running interference to avoid an encounter with the local populous. A member of my team has already crossed the line. While rehearsing problem solving repeatedly in training classes, she never really mastered controlling her own anger. "A bad omen," she mumbles while staring at the ground and fearing he will be a constant source of aggravation rather than a viable asset. She paces back and forth while still in the diner parking lot and worries that dealing with Frank may be a sign of things to come.

As in most cases, when a Lopus becomes upset…I mean really out of sorts with its environment…an enormous amount of adrenaline rushes through its body. The frustration affects their metabolism and their unique ability to change…and to put it simply–change just happens.

Thick brown fur creeps up the back of her neck, while also covering her extremities, her body and finally, her face. Long claws grow out from her fingertips and then, protruding fangs thrust their way out of her widening mouth. Her temper rises and so does she. A dark gigantic bear-like creature appears before all. It towers over Frank with daunting outstretched hands. It yanks him up by the shoulders, proceeds to shake him and forces his large feet to dangle like a rag doll in the wind.

"Are you crazy?" is what she intends to say. However, the only thing coming out of her mouth is a long resounding roar. "Is this how collaborating with you is going to be? Should I send you back now or in the morning?" she booms, all the while, wanting to believe she is getting her point across. And she is—in a way.

The patrons and servers scramble for cover behind nearby cars, trash dumpsters, and even a fire hydrant, when, suddenly, the screams of nearby sirens startle the beast. The metamorphosis reverses as quickly as it began. And the coarse brown fur quickly recedes into nothingness, along with long claws and fangs. Cally's back to her original size, but only after terrifying every person—homeless and otherwise—loitering and lurking in and around the diner.

"Frank! Oh Frank! Are you all right?" cries Terry while scampering to his aid. He staggers about in circles, desperately trying to regain his equilibrium.

Terry steadies him while keeping a suspicious eye on Cally. The Council did not mention anything about numerous capabilities of the Lopus species. The group had suspected the Council nominated her head of the expedition for good reason, but this transformation is unexpected.

"I'm sorry," he grovels. "I slipped…It won't happen again…I promise," he stutters while trembling and wondering whether this is how working with Cally on earth will always be.

Frank hoped to experience a few adventures he would be proud to share with his children and grandchildren alike. However, at this moment he has his doubts about this ever occurring with a creature like Cally at the helm.

"Well, I might as well say what I'm thinking since you can read our minds too!" Terry snaps while bolting to her feet.

"You were out of control just now and I bet at least a dozen humans saw you showing off your powers," she sneers. Her knees are trembling. "I bet the Council would love to hear about this," she scowls while turning up a stiff snout. She is risking it all now and slips defiant hands on both hips. "And you know how much we Lizaradactiles must eat. That is just how we are made you know." Terry's voice quivers as she struggles to hold back tears.

Cally forces herself to admit that Terry's argument is valid. She should have attended more anger management classes offered by the Council prior to the mission. Instead, she allowed herself to become too busy with the to-do-list of endless chores.

"You're right…I was wrong…I apologize," Cally concedes and graciously holds one hand out for Frank to shake.

Frank is leery and bewildered about the hand coming towards him. After all, he reasons, those are the hands that just shook me senseless.

"You're supposed to shake it like we were all taught to do in Human Customs Class," Cally cordially reminds with one hand still extended towards him.

"Oh, yes," he timidly smiles, then, reciprocates. "I remember now." His eyelids flutter like that of a young girls to all of their amusement. Terry giggles.

"That's my Snuggles," Terry drools and gives him a bear hug combined with a sloppy kiss that flushes the cheeks of both Cally and G. W. Carver.

In an attempt to dismiss all concerns, Cally calmly makes mention of her location miscalculations.

"Our contact lives in Denver near the airport. If we hurry, we should be able to make it before dawn."

Before leaving, Cally tosses, what appears to be, a black ping-pong ball into the crowd gathering behind them.

Perplexed onlookers blink in the fog-like mist surrounding them and cough from the strong fumes brought about by, what interstellar travelers commonly call, a memory mixer. It has successfully wiped out any memories of the giant bear-like creature and the events surrounding its appearance.

Cally assures herself that all is well and triumphantly struts towards the road leading to the highway.

"This way!" she shouts. They all lined up behind her.

In the middle of the mêlée, G. W. Carver was thrown to the ground. As a silent observer, he decided to record the entire incident. Away from suspecting eyes, he covertly sends footage to an individual who is not affiliated with the Council or with his group of travelers.

# CHAPTER 4

# MEETING THE AMBASSADOR

Moments before daylight, Cally waits with great anticipation to meet her first human contact. She hopes to develop a noteworthy relationship with this human since the Council assured her he will receive them with open arms. His predecessors were all great hosts and worked well with every liaison sent to earth.

She sends a mental stamp to their human host as they round the last corner near his apartment. It states:

"The Ambassadors have arrived."

The beauty of the Rocky Mountains warm her heart. The rising sun shining upon the mountain range project a myriad of colors. Deep down she desires this to be a sign of good things to come for the inhabitants of this world.

The brick apartment building is four stories high. Cally reaches the third floor long before Frank and Terry. She suspects they're hunting prey. Along the way to Denver the birds were plentiful. The man at the door is taller than she is and looks surprised to see her. "May I help you?" he asks. She is almost at a loss for words. And she wonders why he doesn't know who she represents. "I'm Cally and I'm from the Council," she says. He looks perplexed. "You know…from up there." She points towards the ceiling. "Oh!" he says. "Sorry…I just woke up." He waves her into the apartment, then, checks the hallway for stragglers. "Are you alone?" he asks. She sits the backpack on a living room chair and Carver jumps out.

"He's little. Quite small." Tom blurts out without thinking about the consequences.

Carver leaps to the counter to face Tom eye-to-eye. "Well…Who do we have here," says Carver. "Weak. Very weak and pampered." He turns to Cally. "I don't think he's up for the challenge."

Cally interrupts. "This is G. W. Carver and he is a viable member of our team." She tells Tom in the most amicable way she knows.

"I apologize. I didn't mean to offend." Tom is nervous. He has already started out on the wrong foot. He has decided to make it up to Carver before he goes back.

Frank and Terry file into the apartment unannounced.

Not bothering to wait for introductions, Frank marches straight for the ceramic spotted owl on the other side of the room. He leaps towards the ceiling above and swoops down to crush it. Frank crushes it, to his surprise, into tiny little pieces. Tom's smile withers into a frown. Cally belches a menacing growl. And Terry, well, she giggles and utters her favorite adopted human expression, "Oops".

Tom suspects he'll need to keep a watchful eye on this alien. So, while the other two aliens have a pow-wow in the dining area, Tom escorts Frank to the refrigerator.

"Eat as much as you like," Tom urges. He reminds himself that his visitor is on a strange planet being entertained by a stranger. And Tom sees that he is apparently very famished. Frank nearly snatches the refrigerator door off its hinges to get to the food. Tom quickly jumps out of the way.

"Frank! Really!" complains Cally. Frank doesn't respond to her words. He simply eats everything in the refrigerator in a matter of minutes.

Tom backs away from Frank for fear he may be eaten next.

"We apologize for Frank's abrupt actions and intend to put everything back in order," Cally promises.

"Yeah," blushes Terry while Frank strips the refrigerator and cupboards bare. "He means well."

Cally instructs Tom to do his shopping for groceries while Frank and Terry sleep. She assures him, they usually retire around sunrise.

"They're nocturnal creatures. And…while they sleep…you'll need to re-stock your shelves," she warns. "When they awake, there had better be food here and lots of it."

Before going to sleep for the day, Frank peers down from Tom's small deck and broods about their host being human. He is wary of the Council's decision to place them in the hands of a human who knows nothing about the needs of alien life forms.

"I'm not impressed," he says.

In Prehisteria, he thinks, I would be enjoying breathtaking views of twin moons. They circle my world every 36 hours. In the cool of the day it has unvarying rainbows. They are always brilliant in color. A cool mist continuously blankets the ground. He sighs. "Now that's beauty." Frank really didn't want to leave his home world. He especially felt guilty about leaving his 10 children in the hands of his parents. Terry, his companion and wife, insisted on coming on this expedition. So, in order to ensure her safety, he came along. He's what most humans would consider, a homebody. Terry, on the other hand, loves to travel and explore. Even so, like iron-striking-iron causes sparks to fly, their love for each other remains sure and is never dull.

"I just want to live, live, live!" Terry tells him whenever he suggests she stay closer to home.

"I wish I were home right now," he whimpers, while shuffling towards the hall closet to join Terry. Once there he discovers she is already asleep.

# CHAPTER 5

# KIDNAPPED

Now that Frank has demonstrated aggressive behavior, Tom won't rest easy until he has plenty of food on hand. Cally is the only alien willing to communicate with him. He could sense, the moment they met, that she's a person he can trust.

Tom doesn't quite know how to take this alien. He reminds Tom of the G.I. Joe doll he had as a kid. And then he thinks about the ramifications of the character he chose to be named after. "I'd rethink that name if I were you," Tom advises.

"It is good to see you two have a lot to say to each other. I have a suggestion," she beams while both Tom and G. W. Carver stand at attention in front of her. "You two should go to the market together for sustenance and I'll stay here to make sure nothing goes wrong while you're away."

That sounds like a good idea to both of them. So, Tom grabs a jacket for himself and backpack for his visitor and heads for the door.

"G. W. Carver and I should be back before you know it," Tom tells her. His chest stick out with confidence. "That's long before Frank and Terry should awaken."

She smiles and politely waves as they get into the Uber car.

"Where to?" demands the driver.

"Simms Grocer," Tom quickly tells the man who steps on the gas before he has a chance to buckle the seat belt.

The ride to the grocers is short, yet, somewhat traumatizing. The driver failed to stop at two stop signs. Tom ducks below the seat when the driver sped into ongoing traffic at the last intersection. Tom is so happy to get out of that taxi, he tosses a tip into the driver's lap. "Keep the change and use it for some driving lesson!" Tom slams the door shut and quickly walks away.

Tom exhales while hoisting the backpack over one shoulder and entering the store. Its early morning, so Tom is able to breeze through the customer free aisles with ease.

"I wouldn't get that if I were you. Its fat content is way too high for human consumption," says G. W. Carver. Tom peruses through the meat section. He wonders how many times this little android will give unsolicited calorie counts.

Tom raises an eyebrow and reminds himself of the mission. "How would you know?" says Tom. "Sausage is one of my favorite foods." He adds another pack of sausage to the cart to spite G. W. Carver. This is the fourth time he has attempted to persuade Tom to put something back.

"I'm simply trying to help you out," G. W. Carver defends.

"Shouldn't you remain inside the backpack. I mean…if someone notices us having a conversation they may decide to call the paddy wagon on me.

"Paddy Wagon?" G. W. Carver wonders and quickly searches his data banks for the meaning. "A nickname given to a vehicle police use for transporting prisoners. First came from the New York Draft riots of 1863," he pauses. "I'll watch and listen for now. It is possible I could possibly learn something from this excursion."

While Tom shops, G. W. Carver tears a tiny hole in the backpack just large enough to slide two human-sized fingers through. Now, he is able to monitor Tom's every move without being noticed and takes the liberty of making a few more suggestions.

"Oh! This is lovely. Absolutely lovely!" he raises his voice while gawking at various fruits and vegetables in the produce section.

"How would you know?" Tom whispers. "You've never even tasted human food before."

G. W. Carver doesn't like that statement from a human. "This human knows nothing," he tells himself. "I beg to differ. Sir…I'll have you know that I've tasted human broccoli at a banquet before and it was delicious." His words are quick, concise and filled with contempt.

"Keep your voice down," Tom cautions when an elderly couple passes by. "Someone may hear you," he whispers again.

G. W. Carver raises his muffled voice again in prideful defiance. "Oh—hush! Just tell them it's a pocket radio," he wryly suggests.

Tom struggles with a wayward cart that insists on going left every time he pushes it to the right. As a result, several shoppers succeed at securing a place in line in front of him at the only open register. While in line, he fidgets with his wristwatch and wonders how his visitors are getting along. The sun has been up for well over an hour now and he fears he won't make it back before Frank and Terry are ready for their next meal. Cally says they've missed their breakfast and probably will wake up sooner than later to eat lunch.

He checks the items in his cart against the list he made and discovers he forgot the butter.

"If I get out of line now…" he complains. "I'll lose my place…I need to get home."

The man behind him overhears his one-sided conversation and graciously agrees to save his place in line. Tom humbly thanks the stranger, carefully places his backpack in the seat of his cart before rushing to the back of the store for butter.

"I'll be back in less than a minute," he promises.

Meanwhile, G. W. Carver wedges himself between the soft napkins and paperback books Tom placed in the backpack earlier to provide added support.

"He'd better be back in one minute like he promised," G. W. Carver grumbles. "Not one second less." He literally counts down the seconds.

A casually dressed, unassuming male glides towards Tom's cart. He's been following Tom throughout the store and is certain no one will notice his stalking presence. After all, he reasons, I don't have a handsome, knock-the-girls-dead kind of face like this jerk does. He combs back brown stringy shoulder-length hair with rugged nail-bitten fingers. Then, he scans the front end of the store through edgy dull gray eyes. No one will ever suspect that anything is wrong, he surmises. The fools! He smiles, then, casually approaches Tom's shopping cart. In one swift move, he pushes the unattended cart forward, and snatches the backpack. His long smooth strides towards the door go virtually unnoticed, even though security cameras keep a watchful recording eye on the man who, by now, is rapidly darting across the store parking lot.

# CHAPTER 6

# IN THE HANDS OF A STRANGER

Inside the bag, a sudden jolt knocks G. W. Carver to his side.

"Tom? You stupid fool!" he scolds. "What do you think you're doing?"

His body bounces up and down, like a coiling spring before plummeting down, head first, to the bottom of the bag.

"Help! Help! You fool!" he screams. "The Council will hear about this! You can bet your last dime they will!" he swears while struggling to free himself from the weight of the books. His calls go unanswered. The sound of pounding feet against pavement causes his stomach to churn with worry and concern. The screeching of tires and the persistent blowing of horns are all tale-tale signs that Tom is no longer carrying his bag. He is in the hands of a stranger who must have abducted him the moment Tom stepped away from the cart for butter.

"You fool!" he gasps at the thought of Tom. "How could any human be so careless," he complains in a panicked voice. He soon calms down and decides to maintain a quiet resolve while in the hands of this stranger. In spite of his predicament, he is confident that his fellow aliens will undoubtedly find him soon.

# CHAPTER 7

# THE VISITORS AWAKE

Terry carefully examines the gold-plated rose imprinted on her fork. She cautiously picks it up with two fingers. She sniffs it with a moist snout. Then, she handles the remaining silverware in the same squeamish manner.

"What's the point? It seems like it slows down the entire feeding process," she concludes just before tossing the utensils into the stainless steel sink. Lizaradactiles eat by holding their prey firmly between both hands. Even at the cultural exchange classes they were required to attend, no one ever expected them to use utensils. Terry and Frank both possess an inexplicable restlessness that prevents them from sitting still for long periods of time. They have a need to be in continuous motion. They always explore like hunters. The goal is always the same. The thrill of the hunt. The reward of the prey.

After the food is eaten, Terry sighs. She is restless and hungry for more food. She leaves the empty kitchen cabinets to join Frank and Cally on the sofa. Cally is preoccupied with the book she's reading. "What you got there?" wonders Terry. Cally doesn't stop reading. This makes Terry all the more curious. "What's that you got there?" she persists.

Cally presses the open book against her chest. Then, she runs a finger up and down the smooth spine.

"I'm studying human nature," Cally explains in a dismissive tone. "They call it *Gone with the Wind*."

Terry squints while attempting to decipher the writing on the book cover. Her snout wrinkles upward as she ponders the significance of reading about humans. Then, her interest quickly dwindles at the distinct sound of crunching behind her. Her love interest is pacifying his hunger by nibbling on popcorn kernels he found in the pantry. Frank is occupying his time with TV. He immensely enjoys watching one minute of this and one minute of that along with commercials in between.

"I'm hungry," she whines.

"May I have some?" she begs and drools at the sight of him crunching down on single uncooked kernels of popcorn.

With his back turned away from her, he draws out a throaty sigh. His love for Terry is boundless, but, when it comes to food, he does not intend to share.

"You're the reason why Tom had to go out for food in the first place. You big oaf!" she accuses.

"Is this not right Cally?" She poses a question, then, nervously states it as fact.

Cally ignores her and doesn't bother to look up from the prized book.

"Cally?" pesters Terry.

Cally chooses to remain deep inside the world of Scarlet and Bret, post-Civil War woes and pre-Civil War charm.

Frank is used to his mate taking matters into her own hands. So, the action she displays next comes at no surprise.

Terry snatches the bag of popcorn kernels from his hands. The force tears it open. Kernels fall out and prance off the floor into the air. They rain down onto the oak coffee table. Then, they sprinkle the surrounding brown suede sofa. She crouches and feverishly stuffs popcorn kernels into her wide mouth. Frank rears back in protest and roars. His roars are heard throughout the entire apartment building. With the swift motion of a lion-in-heat, he lunges forward to tackle her from behind. While the two of them exchange blows, a wild fist smashes into Cally. The book topples to the floor.

"Stop! You two stop it now!" Cally screams while jumping to her feet.

Terry finally has her undivided attention, though she didn't intend to get it this way.

"Cut it out right this instant!" she yells again as their fighting escalates.

Frank's whirlwind of revenge frightens Terry into a defensive howl. It's so loud and so high-pitched that it nearly cracks the windows. It does, however, shatter the dining room's faux crystal chandelier. Frank knocks the love seat over onto its backside. He even threatens, more than once, to eat Terry alive.

"I'll eat you alive if I have to!" he shouts.

A dwarf grandfather clock quickly becomes Terry's next weapon of choice. She hisses, then, growls moments before crushing it over his hard-as-a-rock head.

"You big Oaf! I ought to eat you too and spit you out again for the buzzards!" she screams.

Frank counters the attack by grabbing the Swiss Miss clock from the end table and smashing it over her head. Cally's attempts to pull them apart are futile. So, when her patience wears thin, her sleek body begins to take on a different shape.

An enormous surge of adrenalin races through every cell in her body. Fur begins to thrusts its way out through every pore. It wraps itself around her smooth well-defined frame and then her 5 feet 8 inches stature gains an added three feet. Everything else grows to mammoth proportions as well, until she looses herself in the creature she has just become. It towers over them, letting out a fierce resounding roar. She reaches down to pull them apart mere moments before Tom opens the door.

# CHAPTER 8

# MISSING IN ACTION

Tom returns home after G. W. Carver is stolen. He doesn't realize the loud disturbance is coming from his apartment until he reaches the third floor. I told you so, is the phrase going over-and-over again in his mind about the uncertain behavior of the Lizaradactiles. He fears Cally may be hurt. Tom rushes in and is startled by a loud roar. "Cally!" he yells over the noise of the commotion.

Broken pottery pieces and crushed glass crunch beneath his shoes. Tom stumbles into the living room and is alarmed by all he sees. There is a large mammoth creature towering over everyone in his living room.

"What the…?" he says. "Really?" While the creature shrinks down into another form, Tom assesses the damage done to his apartment. To his amazement, the terrifying creature transforms into the alien known as Cally. In case he had any notions about her not being an alien, all of that is dispelled now. She is a genuine creature from another world.

"What in the world is going on here!" he cringes, all the while shaking his head about the debris of broken clocks and shattered glass scattered throughout his apartment. "Couldn't you two at least wait one hour for food?" he snaps.

"No!" Frank tells him and Terry agrees without hesitation.

"We could not wait!" she pouts.

Cally cowards over to Tom and pats him on the back. "Don't worry human," she comforts. "We'll clean this up and replace everything that is broken."

"How?" he whines. "These clocks were from my grandfather!"

"We have our ways," she calmly assures.

He wonders whether the mission has failed before it even had a chance to begin. Given the circumstances, he thinks he should send the aliens back to the Council to choose another ambassador.

Cally looks his way and shrugs her shoulders at the mess. She gives him a gentle smile and uses her powers of telepathy to send him thoughts that soothe his fears and renew his confidence.

Years of preparation has taught me to expect the unexpected, he thinks. I guess we just need to keep moving forward. He realizes that all of the complaining in the world won't clean up this mess. So, without hesitation, he grabs the vacuum and begins cleaning it up himself.

He vacuums a clear path to the French door leading to the deck and steps over debris along the way. Then, he yanks the door open to inhale the cool mountain air. The Aliens follow-suit and fall-in behind Tom by feverishly picking up broken pottery pieces and any other items thrown about during the brawl.

Later on, Tom doesn't question why putting away the groceries is such a breeze and he surprises his self by preparing their meal in record time.

While his back is turned, Cally waves her arms and all of the broken pieces begin to swirl together. The pieces form into their original shapes and effortlessly return to their pre-altercation positions.

"Are those the groceries?" Frank and Terry wonder while staring at the bags left on the kitchen counter. Their mouths water and Frank even drools over the thought of eating fresh prey.

"Oh! No you don't," Cally quickly chides and decides to enlist Frank to help raise the sofa to its original upright position.

She knows all too well their need for nourishment, even so, she is determined to safeguard their host and train them to do things the human way.

"We'll clean up the rest of it," she promises Tom. "You just prepare the food," she urges while giving him a heart felt smile and reassuring nods.

When they finally finish the arduous task of cleaning, the only thing still out of place is the snowy-screen on the TV.

Tom overlooks the queasy feeling in his gut and works up enough courage to break the news about G. W. Carver to them. There is a time and place for everything, so, he decides to tell them about the kidnapping while gathered at the table.

"May I have everyone's attention?" Tom requests while standing to his feet at the head of the table.

Terry plops down onto the only armed chair at the table in a feeble attempt to get back at Frank. He told her earlier that he wanted to sit in the armed chair. Her nose wrinkles up at him in the usual dismissive manner. Only, this time, he has already decided to ignore her antics for the duration of their stay on earth. He also is determined to maintain a good attitude regardless of the circumstances.

"Move your buns!" Cally orders and squeezes in between Frank and Terry with a side chair. "No more arguing on my watch," she scowls.

"This is not easy for me to say–" Tom hesitates while avoiding direct eye contact with them all. "G. W. Carver is missing," he gulps while studying the blank expressions on their faces for any signs of forgiveness.

"What? We just got here!" Terry exclaims. "I mean–," she checks her attitude and calmly asks. "How did it happen?" She has an uncanny knack for overstating the obvious. Even so, she usually asks the questions everyone else is thinking.

"He's such a little fellow," Frank sympathizes. "We need to find him. Who would want to hurt such a little fellow?" he whimpers while turning towards Cally as if she has the solution.

Cally stands to her feet and breaks her stunned silence with: "How? Why? What happened?"

"I'm sorry," he apologizes. "I only left him for a moment. It was a thief," he pauses. "A thief took my bag!"

Cally's first reaction to the news is to pace back and forth on the tiled floor. Then she wails in her native tongue, "Blab la me. Blab la me!" Translation: What a jerk!

Heavy wheezing and an occasional cough are the only expressions coming from Frank. It's his way of expressing grief and displeasure. Frank overlooks the annoyance of his mate's heavy leg resting on one of his knees. He'd rather concentrate on slowing his heavy breathing enough to comment on Tom's unwanted news.

# CHAPTER 9

# JILTED AT LAST

The merciless bouncing has ceased and G. W. Carver clandestinely sits up in the backpack. With one eye pressed against the quarter-sized hole he made earlier, he scans the surrounding area. Passing echoes of life invade his nylon shelter. His capturer snakes his way through the afternoon crowd. In a moment of despair, G. W. Carver's knees quiver. He suddenly gasps at the thought of never seeing the light of day again. He crumbles down to his knees and cringes in anger at the thief.

"Pull yourself together. You moron!" he chides himself. He struggles to pull his body up to the hole once again. "Now, let's see what I can see through this handy hole," he whispers. "I'll attempt to take a look at this poor excuse of a human being who obviously preys on the defenseless." G. W. Carver angles his head just right to catch a glimpse at the thief. He appears to be looking up towards a large building.

"I've always wanted to see inside this joint," Chris Taggard says aloud. He starts up the wide stone steps, then, pauses to read the sign posted above it. It reads: *Mount Harmon Baptist Church, All are welcome.*

"No one will be smart enough to follow me in here," he boasts while stroking a scraggly beard. Taggard cautiously steps into the motif-laden foyer. The scent of shellac and and the smell of aged wood cause him to cringe. It reminds him of one of many foster homes he's lived in as a child.

The sun beams light onto the foyer from the skylights above. The disturbed dust cyclones around and dances in the rays. He reaches into the light to trouble the natural order of nature. Then, Taggard reaches into the bag with one hand. Like the baited line of a fisherman, his hand drops down into the backpack in search of the first catch-of-the-day. A sweaty palm feels its way over the tissue box, the paperback book, until, finally, it slithers around G. W. Carver's waist. G. W. Carver's body stiffens as his capture lifts him up and out of the bag. Before Taggard has a chance to take a closer look at the doll, it becomes rod-iron hot and burns his palm. He stomps and swears from the excruciating pain. In a rage, he shakes the flaming-hot doll loose from his hand. He flings G. W. Carver into the adjacent brick wall and slams the backpack onto the floor. The force of the impact does more than stun G. W. Carver…It knocks his circuits offline which renders him unconscious.

"All of that work for books and a doll," Taggard curses. With shifty gray eyes darting all about, he rejoins the hustling, bustling crowd in search of his next victim.

# CHAPTER 10

# THE SEARCH BEGINS

Cally and Frank clean up the kitchen while Tom and Terry attempt to repair the TV.

She appears to be amused by the way Tom spits out orders at her.

"Screw driver!"

"Check," replies Terry.

"Pliers!"

"Here you go," she giggles.

"Wire!" he shouts while furiously screwing something back into the back of the TV. He's not an electrical engineer, but, he's always been confident that he can fix almost anything.

"Okay–Plug it in!" he orders while standing back to watch the screen.

Terry waddles to the wall. She forces the plug into the outlet. Tom swears at the black lifeless screen.

"I give up," he sighs. His shoulders sag as he makes his way to the sofa. Frank graciously scoots over for him.

"Are you sure?" giggles Terry while making her way to the back of the TV.

"What do you think you're doing?" Tom wonders aloud.

"Just be patient," she giggles again, then, points a finger at her chest. "I fix," she confidently assures him in her usual choppy English.

Terry doesn't ask for tools like Tom did. As far as he can tell, she simply moves her hands around the back of it. Standing to her feet, Terry gives the TV a gentle pat. The TV begins to display a perfect picture along with perfect sound. Tom is dumbfounded. Cally gives an exhausting sigh of relief. The TV is the one thing that has kept Frank and Terry pre-occupied ever since their arrival. She doesn't want to lose her only sitter.

"Now…" Cally takes a break from washing dishes to make an effectual plea. "Can we go look for G. W. Carver?"

"Right," Tom quickly agrees. "There's no time to lose."

Moments later, he leads Cally back to the store where G. W. Carver was taken. He hopes retracing his steps will provide enough evidence to find their littlest visitor.

The parking lot of the store has plenty of activity. A health fair of some kind is taking place and has the one store security guard thoroughly occupied. Getting anyone to remember the incident is like pulling teeth though. After a lot of probing, the store manager tells Tom and Cally that he saw someone rush out of the store, but, he didn't ask why.

"He darted past me so fast…I'm not sure whether I saw a backpack in his hand or not," recalls the store manager. "It's all a big blur," he tells them with a quiver of uncertainty in his voice. "Oh yes!" he recounts while being excited over remembering another detail. "The parking lot security guard may be able to shed some light on the situation. I'll call to see who was on duty this morning."

Tom's heart leaps against his chest at the breaking news. Even so, his joy is quickly overshadowed by the fact that he dropped-the-ball. He recalls his grandfather warning him repeatedly about the seriousness of this mission. He let his guard down. He allowed himself to be distracted for one moment. Now he's suffering the consequences of it in the worst way. "How could I have been so irresponsible?" he scolds himself aloud. "They came to this world as ambassadors of goodwill. I failed them miserably on their very first day." He fears this opportunity and privilege may slip through his fingers because of one careless act.

# CHAPTER 11

# PURPOSE REVEALED

Tom was first provided proof of his grandfather's secret on his 21st birthday. Before that memorable day, he saw Grandfather Bert as a senile old-fart who decided to live out his last days in a world filled with fantasy. He recalls every detail of that day. It changed his perspective on life forever:

As his 21st birthday draws nearer, Grandfather Bert becomes more adamant about sharing details on how to care for aliens. His grandfather grooms him for this extraordinary task by providing Tom with enough books to fill a 12-foot high wall of bookshelves. He has read, "How to please an Alien," 3 times already and religiously quotes highlights during their discussion.

"None of it makes any sense, Grandpa," he use to whine. However, his love for his grandfather far outweighed proving the validity of all he was told. His grandfather finally makes a believer out of him on the night of his birthday celebration.

"Now Tom," Grandfather Bert said. "I know how difficult it has been for you throughout the years to believe in an old-fart like your Grandpa. But, now that you're 21, I feel it's time to show you some proof you can sink your teeth into."

With that said, he leads Tom to the old shed in the back of his home. Tom smirks at his grandfather fumbling with a cluster of keys. When the right one is picked out, he inserts it into the sturdy padlock dangling from the worn metal handle. They both cringe as the bottom of the door scrapes against a concrete floor. With one forceful shove, Grandpa Bert closes the door. The old door is expanded beyond its wooden frame, causing Grandpa Bert to force it open then shut. Grandpa Bert's one flashlight shines a spotlight on spider web covered toolboxes. The light moves across the walls to reveal partially rolled garden hoses, dirt-dusted shovels and numerous rakes. Then, Grandpa Bert locks them inside the shed. Tom is curious about all the secrecy. He patiently waits as his Grandfather uses a heavy-duty padlock to seal the door. Nothing peaks Tom's interest in the least until glimmers of light from white painted windows illuminates an old dusty trunk. It's tucked beneath the only workbench in sight. "What I'm about to show you must be kept secret," he instructed while lowering his voice. "No one else must ever know, not even your Mom and Dad. And, you must promise to conceal this information from your wife, should you ever decide to marry." His grandpa pauses to give Tom time to think things over. "Promise me," his grandfather demanded while grabbing hold of Tom's shoulders and looking him straight in the eyes. Tom was surprised by his grandpa's strong grip. He was certain it was unusually strong for an elderly man. Tom steps away to reclaim his personal space. "No problem," he responded in haste. "I promise to keep your secret. What's the big hush, hush, secret?" Tom had a way of making his Grandpa smile when nobody else could. Tom steps aside while Grandpa Bert unexpectedly kneels down in front of the workbench. He brushes away pesky spiders, then, strains to reach a medium-sized chest. It could've easily be mistaken for a hidden pirate's treasure chest. Once again, Grandfather Bert fumbles through his keys and matches the rather large hole in the padlock with a skeleton key. He opens it like a man with a purpose, then, rummages through the angel-hair straw. Moments later, he pulls out the item he was searching for.

"A clock?" Tom wondered aloud. "All of this for a clock? It's an old-fashion clock with hands on it." Grandfather Bert stands to his feet to face his beloved grandson. "Not just any clock," he said while holding the clock securely between aged hands. "This is a clock full of history like eyes have never seen before," he explained with a sparkling gleam in his, otherwise, dull gray eyes. "This clock is a seer. It actually will show you the proof you've been waiting for."

Grandfather Bert manually turns the hands on the clock counter-clockwise. This prompts the hands to turn on their own and, then, in an instant, they're both submerged into 3D images. The images are illuminated by a spectrum of light emanating from the clock itself. Colorful video footage of the earth's history appears before their eyes. A collage of video footage depicting the earth's future scrolls before their eyes. All of humankind has been influenced by visitations from so-called "extraterrestrials" since time began. From the shaping of the first wheel to the harnessing of power for electricity; from the invention of refrigeration to the discovery of the atom; from the first moon walk to the advancement of mass communications, aliens have kept a watchful eye on our societies. These advanced creatures have looked on with great anticipation for the day humankind would evolve enough to finally meet them face-to-face. They have lived among us in the least likely forms. They have resided among the destitute and poor of our cultured societies. They are the downtroddened misfits of the world today and have been for some time now. They have been the triers of hearts and, in many instances, humankind has failed miserably. Instead of love, they have been met with disdain and abuse. They have been the shackled and abused around the world. They have been murdered and maimed and left on trash heaps to die. These hidden ancient ones will visit Earth one last time to test the hearts of humankind. If the humans fail to measure up to their standards of love, well..," he pauses. "Lets simply pray that we will past the test. The consequences will simply be too great to imagine."

Tom is enamored by the clock and can't seem to take his eyes off of it. "It reveals that the first contact with his family bloodline occurred in Alabama. Tom's great-great-great-great-great grandfather was the contact. He was a scientist around the turn of the 17th Century, however, he made his living as a blacksmith. He always was ridiculed for his belief that man would someday walk on the moon. He was run out of town for saying that he could see God in the stars. Then, the torch was passed on to his son. For some reason, Tom notices, several generations were skipped until contact was made with Tom's grandfather. Then, another strange phenomenon occurred. His father was passed over and Tom himself was chosen to be host to the next celestial ambassadors.

Since this mind boggling revelation, Tom understands the importance of his mission and carries the same burden his ancestors shouldered. The books reveal that aliens have waited for humankind's finite understanding to expand enough to unlock the possibilities of the universe within every human's heart. They have waited for us to mature enough in our spirits to comprehend. We are to comprehend, if at first in only a minuscule measure, the higher powers who rule and reign in the Universes. Only then will humans be equipped to accept outside help to protect them against the impending doom Earth will soon face. An invasion against this planet is imminent. This forces the great Interplanetary Council of Aliens to come up with a plan to prevent it. Thus, with this knowledge in mind, the Council periodically dispatches Ambassadors to earth in order to gather information about the current status of the inhabitants. The Council poses these questions about Earth: Can they defend themselves? Are they aware of the existence of life beyond their stratosphere? And lastly: Will they all gladly receive outside help for their overall defense?

# CHAPTER 12

# CLUES

Ryan Smith, the store security guard, tugs on the starched neckline of his navy shirt while clearing his throat.

"Sure, I saw a guy dart through the parking lot," says Smith. "But, before I could do anything about it, he disappeared down that street," he explains while pointing towards the street in question and clearing his throat again. "I can't go chasing after every Tom, Dick, and Harry running through my parking lot."

"You've told us enough," Cally calmly responds. She signals for Tom to end the conversation.

"Thanks a lot," Tom tells the man. "You've helped us, you really have."

Cally loosely pulls Tom by the sleeve and steers him towards the parking lot.

"We don't have time for talk," she hurries him along by pushing him towards the escape route in question. Meanwhile, she attempts to pinpoint the direction this thief traveled through Extra Sensory Perception (ESP).

"Where do we go from here?" asks a bewildered Tom. "We don't have much to go on, now do we?"

She ignores his fretting and steps up her pace a bit.

"Don't give up so easily," Cally scolds. "I sense G. W. has been here and he's okay for now."

Cool breezes nip at her nose as she leads the way through residential streets.

"The downtown business district is just up ahead," Tom shares.

Cally's not interested in the community that lies ahead. She is simply determined to find G. W. Carver. What will the Council think if I can't find him, she worries?

Moments later she glances over her shoulder expecting to see Tom and hear his heavy breathing. To her dismay, Tom is not in sight. This forces her to backtrack until she finds him leaning against a light pole and breathing heavily.

"Are you okay?" she asks while gently rubbing a hand up and down his back.

"I'll be all right…just give me a minute to catch my breath."

"Should I go on without you?" she wants to know.

"Uh…Well we need to come up with a different strategy that doesn't include walking."

# CHAPTER 13

# A GIRL FINDS THE BACKPACK

As has been the case lately, Kashonda is too tardy to eat her Sunday morning breakfast.

"Girl..!" her grandmother scowls. "You better get down here! Child...I don't want to be late again," she declares in a lazy southern drawl.

Kashonda Leonard grabs a breakfast bar from the pantry before joining her grandmother in the car.

"Why an 11-year-old girl has got to spend so much time in front of a mirror, I'll never know," her grandmother complains while backing out of the driveway. "And after your choir finishes singing, I expect you to join me in the pews this time.

"Yes ma'am," Kashonda reverently responds.

Kashonda adores and cherishes her Grandmother Matilda. Kashonda was merely 5-years-old when Matilda first came to live with her family. Grandfather Leonard passed away in the tiny town of Carrollton, Georgia. They lived as sharecroppers for most of their lives. Denver is a big place to relocate to for someone from such a small community. Just the same, as far as Matilda Leonard is concerned, time, people, and every living creature must bow down to her wishes. She manages the best of Denver with her wit, charm and what she refers to as—good old-fashioned southern hospitality. She bakes fresh rolls, biscuits, and cakes for friends and family members. You name it, she can bake it. And, she makes sure that everyone on their block has tasted her goodies. Her cooking is such a big hit that her daughter-in-law's co-workers have offered to lend her money to open a bakery.

"If I had your baking skills I'd be as rich as Martha Stewart by now," says Cecilia, a co-worker of Betty, Matilda's daughter-in-law.

"Betty, tell your mother-in-law a thing or two about how the rich do it," Cecilia says one day right in front of Matilda.

"Matilda honey, you need to let me set you up," she suggests.

Even so, Matilda doesn't like someone younger than she is meddling into her affairs. And she especially doesn't care to be called by her proper name without putting a title in front of it.

"It's Mrs. Matilda to you young lady," she corrects.

Matilda is old-school and does not intend to change for the people of Colorado.

Kashonda doesn't understand her grandmother's old-fashion ways, but, she has decided to give her an A for effort since she spends more time with her than her parents do.

"Don't forget to get your choir robe out of the back," Matilda reminds while Kashonda steps out of the vehicle. She promised to drop Kashonda off at the church for choir rehearsal even though she has other things to do. She is a woman of her word and no sacrifice is too great for her only grandchild.

"Awe…Smells delightful," Kashonda says after removing the freshly dry-cleaned choir robe out of the SUV. She holds the purple robe up to her nose and deeply inhales. "It smells fresh off the press." Kashonda loves the smell of dry cleaning and prefers it over her grandmother's objections. Matilda complains that dry cleaning is throwing away good money and repeatedly reminds Kashonda that hand washing garments will get them cleaner.

"Shoot, I'll hand wash and iron it for free," Matilda tells her.

"Now Grandmother..," Kashonda cunningly replies. "Allow me this one pleasure in life."

Matilda always responds, "That's what your father always says and girl, you are just like him."

Kashonda gives her grandmother a gentle peck on the cheek. Then, she makes the ascension up the stone steps while handling her robe like a glass slipper.

The choir director patiently waits while Kashonda changes into her robe.

"You ready to sing, my little songbird?" asks Billy David, the choir director.

"What do you mean— Songbird?" she blushes.

Billy glides towards her, only stopping when his protruding belly acts like a buffer between them.

"Have you kept your solo a secret?" he anxiously asks.

"Of course I have," she assures him.

"Good," he exhales and appears to be more excited about her first solo than she is.

"I want you to blossom like a flower," he twirls. "Sing like a nightingale…" he sings. Then, he slides to the left and twist to the right while whirling his XX-large frame around. Billy moves to a beat only he can hear. Kashonda smiles as he rolls chubby dough-boy hands towards his robust belly. While keeping time with the beat, his feet scratch and tap the floor like a hen in a chicken coop.

"Give it your all! Don't hold back! Don't be afraid to hit those high notes either!" His voice goes up a few octaves while demonstrating the sound. "Oh yeah!" his voice screeches.

"Got to go meet with the rest of the choir," he announces before abruptly waddling towards the adjoining choir room.

She wets her dry throat with a sip of bottled water. It is cool and refreshing and at room temperature, which is according to Billy's explicit instructions. He always demands his singers protect their voices above all else. He constantly warns, "Ice cold water and singing is a recipe for disaster."

While the sanctuary fills, Kashonda nervously glances through a break in the curtains behind the stage. Most of the parishioners have already found seats and anxiously wait for the Service to begin. Since Mount Harmon Baptist Church finished renovating the main sanctuary, their membership has skyrocketed. Kashonda is just grateful to be able to sing. She counts the downtown Denver location as an added bonus. She and her friends in the suburbs don't get to see very many city lights out there. Now, she gets to be a part of the city lights every weekend. While hurrying back to the choir room, she nearly stumbles over a backpack lying on the floor.

"Hey! What's this?" she wonders aloud while cautiously picking it up by one strap. "I know this doesn't belong here." A tap on the shoulder interrupts her thoughts. Kashonda drops the bag to the floor. Julie, another second soprano member of the choir, picks it up.

"What are you doing out here?" Kashonda wonders.

"Billy sent me to find you. It's time to sing," she expresses while waving long slinky arms through the air like a music director.

"Here's your bag," Julie holds the bag up to Kashonda at eye level. She too is bubbling over with excitement over Kashonda's gifted voice. Julie peers down at her friend who takes the backpack and carefully slings it over one shoulder. With Kashonda's talent, Julie and others are certain to win the choir competition this year.

"Okay, let me just find out who this bag belongs to first," Kashonda tells her.

"I don't think so," Julie retorts while guiding her by the shoulders to the choir room.

"Well, at least let me put it in my locker," Kashonda insists.

Julie folds her arms in front of her while stepping out of Kashonda's path. She's determined to watch over Kashonda until she makes it to the choir loft.

In the meantime, G. W. Carver wakes up to the horror of being surrounded by darkness. The sudden sounds of music and singing startle him as well.

"How did I get here?" he mumbles. "Where is here?"

He knows the last thing he remembers is flying through the air by the hands of that awful man. Then, everything else is a big blur.

"Get me out of here!" he panics while groping at the air and struggling to breathe. His muffled yells for help go unanswered and soon he comes to the realization that no one will come to his aide. More importantly, he realizes that no one must discover he is not a real doll.

"What am I doing? No one must know that I'm alive. No one must know I exist," he tells himself while snuggling back in between the tissues and books.

He waits in the darkness, not knowing where he is or who is holding him captive this time.

# CHAPTER 14

# THE SEARCH CONTINUES

Strong gusts of wind stir-up brittle autumn leaves while a perfect formation of squawking geese fly overhead. Lingering traces of G. W. Carver's scent lead them through the liveliest business district of Denver. Here, the blare of honking horns and screeching tires are common sounds, especially during morning rush hour. Cally raises one hand in an effort to stop an oncoming car. The driver abruptly stops, then, yells out of his window while passing by, "Baby I'll stop for you anytime!" She is pleased to know that fact and nods at him approvingly. She's oblivious to the fact that he is simply flirting. Tom beckons her to come back to the sidewalk he's standing on, but, she ignores his gesturing and continues to cross. Her careless action creates a traffic jam and gets the unwanted attention of an officer on horseback.

"Stop!" he shouts. "You can't cross there!" Tensions rise. "What's wrong with you lady? Don't you see the no-crossing sign and all this dam traffic?"

Unshaken by his irritation and threat to arrest her, she quickly keys in a code into the devise on her wrist. In an instant, the business district is without sound and motion. Mouths open, yet, remain silent. Pedestrians freeze in mid-stride while the belching smoke of automobiles suddenly becomes suspended in mid-air. Tom rushes past a woman and stops to wave a hand in front of her face. He wonders: Is she breathing? He jostles her shoulder bag and smiles. Just then, he notices that Cally is almost out of sight.

"Hey– Wait up!" he calls while running to catch up.

"Amazing!" he says with renewed vigor and optimism about Cally's time altering device. "It's absolutely incredible! You have to let me in on your secret!"

No matter how much he probes, she has no intention of sharing the secret with him or any other human.

They press on at stealth speed, from block-to-block, down one street after another, towards G. W. Carver's location.

# CHAPTER 15

# G. W. CARVER MEETS KASHONDA

Back at the church, expectations are high. The burden to perform perfectly in front of peers, friends, and family members rest solely on her shoulders. Billy summons Kashonda to step forward with the wave of a hand. Shaky legs take her to the podium. She fumbles with the microphone until it leaps out of its holder and pops her smack dab in the middle of her forehead. In Kashonda's eyes, the church full of people suddenly becomes a room full of blurred spectators. They stare. She hears heavy breathing and suddenly realizes it is hers. Her prayers for a miracle to get her out of the spotlight go unanswered. The program begins.

"You can do it girl. I have confidence in you," Billy encourages from the choir loft behind her.

Kashonda reminds herself of the reason for being there in the first place and it works. She is not there to entertain, but instead, she is there to sing praises to her God. From here on out, she tells herself, I'm going to sing whether my body wants to or not. Immediately, she blocks out the low drum of noise around her, opens her mouth, and sings with everything that is within her. Suddenly, she feels like she's in another plain of existence. She closes her eyes and soars high, then, low. She soars over peaks and down into valleys. She stretches out both arms while singing an impossibly high note, then, slowly presses them back onto her 5'2" frame. This is her first solo performance outside of the bedroom and she intends to make the best of it. With feet firmly planted on the wood floor, she sings a soulful gospel tune. It flows from her innermost being and perfectly compliments the choir, who, at the direction of Billy, sway from side-to-side.

Clara Jones, a steady churchgoer, taps Matilda on the shoulder. Matilda hates being tapped at all and cuts an eye at Clara.

"That's your granddaughter…Isn't it?" Clara wants to know.

"Yeah-Yes," Matilda hesitates. She didn't know her granddaughter was going to lead a song. She never even heard her sing before. "Yes," she composes herself as pride rises to her throat. "…And I have to tell you…I'm just as surprised as you are."

"Amen, all right!" shouts Clara Jones while waving an embroidered handkerchief towards the choir.

"You sing that song child!" approves another woman while jumping to her feet as fast as a moving projectile.

One congregation member after another raises their hands in praise to God because of the beautiful sounds coming from Kashonda. The loudest of the praises though are coming from Matilda's corner. She not only stands and shouts, but, she takes a bold step into the center aisle to make her pleasure known to all.

"That's my grandchild!" she yells above every other cheerer. As far as Matilda is concerned, no one is going to praise her granddaughter louder than her.

Kashonda is not as distracted as she thought she would be by the praises coming from the audience.

"I once was lost, but now I'm found…Ooh-ooh," her voice resounds throughout the rafters.

The melodious tune flows down narrow aisles like rose peddles on a slow moving stream.

"I was bound, but now, I'm free…Ooh-ooh…Yeah…Yes," she sings while standing tall and erect, just like Billy coached her to do. Her voice is smooth and raps around the audience like warm ribbons of velvet.

After the service, Matilda scans the choir loft and the surrounding area for her granddaughter. She notices Clara coming her way and attempts to dodge her by cutting through the pews to reach an exit. She knows from experience and old-fashioned common sense that Clara Jones is simply a busybody and not a true friend at all.

"Where's your granddaughter?" asks Clara while cornering her in the middle aisle.

"I certainly can't leave here without telling her how much I enjoyed the singing. It was beautiful, absolutely beautiful!" she says through a witchy giggle.

"I don't know. She…" Matilda stutters before Clara cuts her off.

"Oh, I know," Clara says. "She must be downstairs taking off her robe. I'll go see." Before Matilda can utter another word, Clara heads for the stairs.

"Hold on now," huffs Matilda, who takes a lot of stuff from people before reaching her boiling point. "You can wait right here with me for *my-y-y* granddaughter," she orders while reaching for her arm. "Better yet," Matilda tells her while backing her into the wall. "You *will* compliment her some other time."

"Ah…You're right Miss Matilda…I didn't mean any harm," she sheepishly apologizes. Matilda keeps a watchful eye on Clara. Matilda wants to make sure she exits the church rather than sneak back in to visit Kashonda.

"So now, I'm Miss Matilda?" she huffs while folding both arms over her stomach.

Meanwhile in the choir room, Kashonda hangs her robe with care by covering it with cleaners plastic. The locker door slams shut behind her when she hurries towards the stairs to join Matilda.

"Oh no!" she panics. "The backpack…I need to get it!"

She rushes back to the locker, lifts the bag from the hook and carries it into the main sanctuary.

"Does this bag I found in the foyer belong to anyone?" she inquires of the few parishioners still lingering in the sanctuary.

She holds it high up in the air for all to see and gets no response. "Okay, maybe I need to use the microphone," she tells herself. "Excuse me please…May I have everyone's attention?" she asks the churchgoers one more time. "I found this bag in the foyer. Does it belong to anyone here?"

Still, no one responds. The Pastor's wife works her way through the crowd to where Kashonda makes her plea.

"Don't worry about that bag. Keep it. If anyone comes looking for it, I'll know where to find it," she assures while giving her a warm embrace.

"That was a beautiful song you blessed us with today. I wish I had a voice like that."

"Oh, thank you ma'am," Kashonda blushes.

G. W. Carver scoffs at their conversation.

"Oh great," he sarcastically chirps.

Kashonda hears him while walking away from the Pastor's wife and peeps into the bag. G. W. Carver stiffens again, becoming as hard as plastic, and as warm as pudding. She lifts the doll out of the bag and takes a closer look.

"You don't look like you can talk," she tells him. "Say something," she commands.

She shakes the doll a few times before placing it back inside the bag.

"Maybe I just imagined hearing you talk."

She shrugs her shoulders, then, heads towards the vestibule to meet her grandmother.

Matilda patiently waits by the red double doors in front of the church. Clara Jones suddenly whizzes by Kashonda without even speaking.

"What in the world is she up to," Kashonda wonders aloud. "Ha! Ha!" laughs Matilda. "She's apparently trying to escape the wrath of her husband."

Johnny, Clara's husband, has the look of fury on his face. He corners his wife next to the bulletin board and shakes a long finger in her face. The couple begins to draw a crowd of onlookers. "I'm sure Clara's meddling has gotten her in trouble again," assumes Matilda. She smiles, then, turns her attention towards Kashonda.

"You're full of surprises little one," she compliments. "I can't wait to tell your parents about your performance today." Kashonda feels a sudden ping of anger against her parents for missing this and mostly every other important event in her life. As far and she is concerned, Grandma Matilda is her mother and father for now. She loves her more than she'll ever know for being here.

# CHAPTER 16

# THE CLUE

Being whisked from one dimension to another is an experience Tom is not likely to forget. Cally had to snatch Tom out of the way of a semi-truck. One second longer and he would've been cream cheese smeared all over the road.

"That was close," he says. "Thanks."

"You're welcome," she replies. "You wouldn't have been the first person I lost that way."

He shakes his head at her comment. "I don't even want to know the details."

They walk and walk and walk until they come to the side of town where the buildings look old and Gothic.

"What's this place?" she wonders while pointing to a church where slate-covered steps lead to a pair of red painted doors.

"It's a church," Tom steps back and answers. He takes a full shot view of the building. Cally senses he's admiring the architectural design of the structure.

"Explain," she abruptly demands.

"People worship God in there. You know, a place where people sing songs, clap their hands and listen to a speaker," he explains in more detail.

"Oh, like sacred? A place for sacrifices?" she wonders. Understanding comes along with the sudden horror of G. W. Carver being sacrificed on a burning altar.

"Oh no!" she shrieks, then, darts up the steps like a fireman anxious to put out a fire. She bursts through the crimson double-wide doors. Then, Tom stumbles up the wide slate steps after her.

He gasps while jumping over the crumbling double doors. "No!" he shrieks. "What are you doing?" he shouts in horror while managing to catch up with her and grab hold of one arm. "I know what you're thinking!" he pulls her towards him to make eye contact. "They don't do that here!"

A middle-aged man wearing a well-tailored navy suit calls out to them from the far corner of the vestibule. A sharply-dressed woman follows close behind as they make their way to Tom and Cally.

"May we help you?" the woman wants to know. Her soothing voice calms the savage beast readying to manifest in Cally.

Lillian Clondyke, the Pastor's wife, intends to ask them about the custom doors lying in shambles at her feet. It doesn't seem possible, she reasons, for a couple as slim as they are, to have the strength to do something like this.

"I hope you two have a good explanation for this!" Pastor John Clondyke tightly demands while squinting at them through dark brown eyes.

Cally's glance quickly drops towards her feet. She regrets acting so rashly. The couple standing before her deserves more respect than this, she thinks. One quick glance Tom's way lets her know that he feels the same. She senses that he is thoroughly disgusted and equally embarrassed by her actions. She decides to do more research into human behavior and intends to apply all she learns to her behavior in the future.

"I guess I don't know my own strength," she sheepishly admits.

Pastor John and Lillian throw doubting glances at each other.

"Now, young lady, I know you were not able to break down those doors by yourself. They have stood for nearly 60 years in that very same spot," claims Lillian while firmly resting petite cinnamon brown hands on both hips.

"We are *so* sorry. We pushed the doors and they simply toppled over. You wouldn't happen to have termites would you?" Tom convincingly implies.

Pastor John scratches the top of his head which is lightly dusted with gray hair.

"Well, we'd like to believe you, but, the police are already on their way. We have a security system you know," he warns.

"Now John," Lillian earnestly responds with a smile. "You know we can simply tell the police we *must* have termites, because, I believe these sweet young people are innocent."

Cally takes Lillian's comment as her queue to leave and does just that. She allows her instincts to take control once again and dashes down the stairwell leading to the choir room.

"Where is she going?" Pastor John warily wonders.

"Do you ask where I'm going when I quietly leave the room?" Lillian defends. She's convinced that Cally must be visiting the ladies' room.

Tom decides to wait for the police to arrive along with Pastor John and Lillian. He doesn't want Lillian to get the notion to join Cally in the Ladies' room since, he suspects, she didn't go there. In the meantime, Pastor John is still suspicious of their motives and keeps a sharp eye on him.

I've been around the block a few times, he thinks while peering down at Tom. I don't believe their story for one minute.

"Why did you and your friend come in here of all places?" he questions. "What can we really do for you two, young man?" he wonders while studying Tom's body language.

Tom clears his throat, which is dry and scratchy from all the activities of the day.

"Well, we suspect that the thief who stole my bag came here for some reason," he explains after concluding that telling the truth in a place like this couldn't hurt.

"What color was your bag?" she wonders.

"It was tan and cloth," he answers. "It didn't have anything of real value to anyone except for my niece. It has her favorite doll inside."

Lillian grabs her husband by the hand.

"Excuse us for a moment," she says while leading him away from Tom to the other side of the room size foyer. "All of this trouble for a bag?" she whispers.

"Well, maybe there is something inside it he doesn't want anyone to know about," he replies.

"A member found that bag earlier today," she confides. "Should we let him know?"

Her husband paces back and forth while contemplating an answer.

"No! Let's tell them we'll call the moment we hear about a bag being found. Then, we can get their number and address," he suggests. "Who has it anyway?"

"I told that nice girl, Kashonda, to keep it until someone comes to claim it," she answers.

"Well," he concludes. "We'll find out what's inside from her before we call this odd couple."

Tom suspiciously studies their expressions when they come back over to him and feels like they're holding something back. He wonders whether G. W. Carver the doll was found or G. W. Carver the alien? He prays their secret has not been discovered?

"Excuse me, Pastors," he says while walking towards the stairwell. "I'll find out what's taking her so long."

Finding Cally was easy. Tom locates her in the basement choir room. He finds her rummaging through things inside the lockers and cabinets.

"We need to get out of here," he urges. "The police are on their way."

"You're right," she reluctantly agrees. "At least I know where to pick up the trail again the next time we venture this way."

The time was well spent, thinks Tom as they climb the stairs leading to his apartment. They both are relieved to find everything is still intact. The Lizaradactiles are sound asleep inside the hall closet

"Everything appears to be in order," he sighs. His reassuring smile gives Cally a warm feeling inside. She stretches her neck around him to view the two sleeping beast for herself. The stress on the wooden coat rod draws her attention. One side of the rod sags more than the other. There is no doubt that Frank is the heavier of the two. Cally is pleased to see them so peaceful while hanging upside-down. She wishes they would remain as docile while awake as well. While taking note of their clawed feet curled around the wooden rods, she concludes it's impossible to fight against nature.

Tom heads for the kitchen and when he opens the refrigerator he finds it completely bare. It's a big relief to both of them since the more the Lizaradactiles eat…the longer they'll sleep. The more they sleep, the less they'll fight and the less they fight, he smiles, the more peace of mind he's likely to enjoy. "Even the butter is gone," he says aloud, then, suddenly leaps in place while doing the two-step touchdown dance.

"Well, you know you have to go shopping before they wake up," Cally reminds while doing a double-take at the sight of him dancing.

"I'll go with you," she insists. "No need for worry," she assures him. "I'm sure we'll be back before they're up and about this time."

# CHAPTER 17

# ONE STEP CLOSER

"It's a good day for travelling," Cally shouts while admiring the snow-capped Rocky Mountain range from the patio window. "You've been in the shower for nearly an hour. Are you alright?" she shouts. She turns back towards the mountains and is captivated by the way snow cascades down from each peak its own unique way. A brilliant spectrum of orange, purple, red and yellow serve as a perfect backdrop for the majestic peaks. In spite of her oath to only use her powers for emergencies, she decides to hurry Tom along. Her thoughts instantly wrap around his. Tom abruptly cuts his shower song short, drys himself off in record time and reaches for the door knob before putting on his clothes. Luckily, he realizes his mistake before exiting the bathroom. Then, he dresses so quickly it completely escapes his memory.

Moments later, he joins her in the living room.

"I know G. W. Carver was held in a locker at that church for a long period of time. Are you sure sacrifices aren't done there?" Cally worries.

Tom slips an arm around her shoulders and gently squeezes.

"I'm positive," he assures.

"I picked up his trail and it led to the back of that building," she quickly adds.

"That would be where the parking lot is," Tom injects.

"That's our ground zero," she concludes. "Let's get started."

"Wait a minute," he demands. "I'll join you under one condition."

"What's that?" she asks.

"Let's take the bus this time."

She agrees.

They quickly make their way to the bus stop located across the street from where Tom lives.

"The bus is late as usual," Tom sighs. They've been impatiently waiting for nearly an hour. Just the same, Tom is determined to wait. The pain of trying to keep up with her is still aching in his feet.

The bus finally arrives. It is carrying a full load, but, the two of them are lucky enough to find two seats together. This early morning express is way more crowded than Tom expected it to be.

Just as they near the heart of downtown, the bus engine begins to putter.

"Is something wrong?" wonders Cally.

"Oh, this guy simply doesn't know how to drive," Tom jokes. Cally's gentle expression turns into a frown.

"No worries," Tom assures. "I bet he was driving long before we were born."

The driver struggles down to a lower gear, and revs the engine a couple of times until it chokes, coughs, then, finally, dies.

"Of all the rotten luck," complains Tom.

All of a sudden, the bus bumps into a curb and causes passenger's heads to jerk back in unison.

"He appears to be having engine problems," Cally notes. "And you inferred his troubles were due to a lack of driving skills." Tom sighs. "I was being sarcastic."

While filing out of the bus, he passes by the driver and gives a sympathetic nod.

"I believe we'll find G. W. Carver soon. Don't you?" she says while searching his face for some sort of reassurance.

"Yes," he hesitates. "Let's hope so."

Tom becomes apprehensive while watching Cally glance at her wrist watch. He hopes she doesn't suggest they walk the rest of the way to the church.

"I have a feeling we'll be waiting here for hours before another bus comes our way," he admits.

She links both arms over her chest and raises an eyebrow. "We may not get back to your apartment in time if we do," she cautions. "You never allow Lizaradactiles go hungry. There's no telling what they'll eat or whom."

Tom expected Cally to come to this conclusion the moment the bus broke down.

"Okay. I get the picture," he concedes. "Let's walk the rest of the way."

# CHAPTER 18

# DISCOVERING HUMANITY

Kashonda scans her spacious bedroom for a secure place to store the backpack. She finally settles on a hook inside the closet door. Everyday it will serve as a reminder that she possesses something that does not belong to her. Returning it to the rightful owner is her goal and she is certain that some little child misses the doll she's holding in her hand.

"Maybe you'll be more comfortable over here next to Barbie and my stuffed animals," she suggests while standing G. W. Carver between them. Her father bought the Barbie doll from Paris long before it hit the shelves in America. She was only seven at the time and ever since then, has loved it more than the rest of her collection. It seems like it was only yesterday, she recalls, while moving Barbie over to make room for the latest addition. She hardly ever sees her Dad since he took that overseas assignment. He's been as illusive as a ghost. Having an airline pilot for a father appears to be such a perk. She'll never tell him that she wishes he had a different career. Kashonda loves him too much to cast a shadow over something he enjoys so much.

"Good night little man," she says to G. W. Carver before closing her eyes for the night.

The next morning, she reaches for the snooze button on her cell phone and knocks over the pink princess lamp. Waking up at 6am is always hard for Kashonda, especially while she's in dreamland. Oftentimes, the dreams are an exaggerated version of future events. Today, she dreams about taking bows for her performance in the Church Choir. She struggles to wake up when suddenly, in the same dream, she is surrounded by tiny green men. Then, the dream ends as quickly as it began.

Because of the dream, she's motivated to begin the day rehearsing a new song for the school choir. She sings while picking out her outfit. She sings in the shower. She sings while getting dressed. And, she even sings while on her way downstairs for breakfast.

In the meantime, G. W. Carver stiffens at the sound of her alarm. She appears to be harmless, he observes. If her voice is pleasant to him, then, he is certain all of the known universe will love it as well. Know your enemy, is what he has learned throughout the years. "Know your enemy. I need to know more about this human who has taken me captive."

The moment he is sure Kashonda has left for the day, G. W. Carver takes this opportunity to look around the room. He jumps down from the three-drawer dresser to the floor. Then, he leaps to the top of her bedpost to explore the book lying on her pillow. He is an excellent jumper. His designer made sure he would be able to jump, leap, and navigate as well as anyone 10 times his size. "B-I-B-L-E," he phonetically spells out the word on the book cover. This book must be a good read, he concludes, since Kashonda read it before dozing off last night.

Within minutes he reads the entire book and finds it compelling. He also concludes that this Bible is a blueprint, a guide for life on earth. "I only hope that humans will learn how to abide by this living blueprint before the war begins," he thinks aloud. Now, he has an appetite for more knowledge. So, he makes his way to the highest piece of furniture in the room and perches himself on top of it. Resting against the dresser mirror, his eyes search the room for more books.

"Ah…There they are."

A five-shelf bookcase is in the opposite corner of the room just waiting to be explored. Within the span of an hour, he reads them all without batting an eye. Reading these books leaves him thirsty for more knowledge about this world that's about to be destroyed.

He's traveled the universe and has even visited planets in different galaxies, yet, he has never read anything as earthy as Tom Sawyer in Huckaberry Finn. He thinks that Anne Frank is absolutely captivating, tragic, yet, triumphant. And Harriet Tubman has just become his true American hero for daily risking her life in order to rescue fellow human beings. "Could slavery exist anywhere else on this planet?" he shudders at the thought. "How brutal."

# CHAPTER 19

# FEEDING TIME

The scanner performs a slow motion waltz while the cashier cautiously and meticulously runs each item over it. There are first time hits and a lot of misses which cause her to repeat the tedious process all over again. Heavy sighing and fleeting looks from disgruntled shoppers don't appear to hasten the process along either. Tom and Cally find themselves at a loss for kind words when their turn to check out finally comes.

"Uh…Hello," the cashier says while glancing up. She takes her time scanning their last item. "Is this yours too?" she asks while reaching for the next item on the counter. With a sigh, they rush out of the store and flag down a taxi.

"Next time I'll simply arrange for an Uber or Lyfe driver," he assures Cally who appears to be somewhere else.

Tom's sinuses react with an incessant flow of sneezing and sniffling to the smell of smoke and worn rawhide. Cally, well, she's not affected by the nuisance at all and casually glances out the back window at the sun slowly setting over the horizon.

"Almost there," she exhales while calmly snuggling down into her seat.

When the time comes for Tom to pay the tip, the driver ends-up wrestling the tip out of his hand. Tom doesn't let go of his money easily these days, not with all of the added expenses straining his meager income.

They safely arrive at his apartment. The hardest part of this trip is carrying the groceries up the steps. The taxi driver did not offer to help with the bags. He watches them unload through his rear view mirror and then takes off like a flash of light.

"Listen," Cally pauses to listen to the sounds on the other side of the door. Tom stops in his tracks. One eyebrow raises at the sound of cooing.

The gurgling coming straight from the other side of the door. Tom's door keys drop to the floor.

"Come on! Hurry!" Cally urges. "I was afraid of this. They're awake."

The door flies open just as Tom leans into the lock with his key. He stumbles, head first, onto the floor. He can't make out the person climbing over him, but he knows it is one of the Lizaradactiles. By the time he recovers to his feet, Frank and Terry had spilled groceries all over the floor.

"We didn't know what we would do had you not come when you did," Terry confesses while tearing into a bag of uncooked rice. "We were contemplating our next move when we heard someone at the door."

In the meantime, Cally retrieves the rest of the bags from the taxi. And Tom, well, he hurries towards the kitchen with Terry on his heels.

"I told Frank it would be too dangerous to go out into this strange world by ourselves. He was planning on finding one of your stores he saw on that machine he likes to watch so much," she explains all the while referring to the TV.

Tom is too busy preparing their next meal to respond.

Frank meets Cally at the door and snatches the bags out of her hands. She growls and he backs down with an apology.

"Sorry," he apologizes. "I'm just so hungry. I mean well, you know how it is. Don't you?"

Cally rushes the remaining bags to the kitchen. "If it were up to Frank" she scoffs. "He'd eat everything in sight, even the brown paper bags."

For the first time in Frank's life, he felt self-conscious about the way he behaved. He suspects the way he feels has something to do with Cally's special powers. He doesn't like it. As a matter of fact, he hates it and intends to fight these feelings with everything that's within him.

Terry looks at Cally and frowns. She worries that her stay on earth may be ruined by Cally's insistence on controlling their every move.

She and Frank were selected to come to earth by the Council out of over 40,000 other applicants throughout the Galaxy. She's not about to have her, once-in-a-lifetime, opportunity foiled over Cally's nonsense.

"Stop fussing with her," shrieks Terry.

"Oh, shut your trap," Frank counters. He picked up that local phrase from watching reruns of *Meet the Browns.* He notices it appears to be very affective on Mr. Brown.

Terry doesn't give him the satisfaction of responding. Instead, she finds pleasure in snatching the bag of raw meat out of his hands. Running interference, Cally steps between them to avoid another altercation like the last one they had when Tom was away.

Less than an hour later, dinner is cooked and served. The long ordeal of shopping, unloading, cooking, cleaning, more cooking, and more cleaning, has worn Tom out.

He's ready for bed and Cally can see it in his eyes.

"Hey," Terry says while resting her clawed feet on the coffee table. "G. W. Carver is still missing. You two haven't said a word about him since you came back," she points out to Cally and Tom who are lounging on the adjacent love seat.

"Cally..," Tom says as if to be directing the question her way. The room becomes deathly silent. Cally begins wringing her hands together. This is something she always does in the face of danger or whenever she is genuinely annoyed.

Tom, well he's a nibbler. It doesn't matter what he has in his hands, he has to nibble on it whenever circumstances become overwhelming. The pencil in his hand now is the object of his nervous affection. It's beginning to look like a badly carved stick rather than a no. 2 pencil. His teeth work their way to the lead tip. They are content to chew there for a while. While pecking, he allows his imagination to carry him to the place G. W. Carver could be.

*Tom imagines G. W. Carver being poked and prodded by an admiring little boy, who eventually decides to decapitate him.*

Suddenly, Tom bites the tip of the eraser completely off.

As Tom deals with his guilt, Frank rubs his tight stomach which is satisfyingly full. He feels great empathy for his pint size colleague and concludes that his friend must be desperately hungry by now. For Frank and all of his species, hunger is a fate far worse than death.

Frank and Terry lean forward and listen tentatively as Tom and Cally recap the events and mishaps of the day. It becomes clearly evident to them both that this task is far too demanding for simply two people. So, Terry persuades them to add her and Frank to the search team.

"I hate to ask you this," Tom says to Cally away from the ears of their associates. "Well...tomorrow is a very important day for me at work.

You will have to go without me," he pauses. "I hope you will take Terry's offer and allow them to go along this one night," he pleads while firmly squeezing her shoulders.

His plea is worth considering, she thinks. We've wasted enough time as it is. Even though this human is our host, she reasons, he doesn't have the innate skills necessary to be of any use to us tonight or any other night, for that matter. The Lizaradactiles will, at least, be able to keep up with my pace, she concludes.

"Cally, I'll give you my cell phone. If anything goes wrong, call me on the landline immediately!" he tells her before retreating to his bedroom for the night.

Tom uses this time to go over his boss, Shakeam Adams, presentation, which is due tomorrow. He almost forgets about his commitment to Shakeam because of the overwhelming events of the day. Tomorrow, Shakeam will deliver his golden presentation and Tom will supply the props. If his presentation looks good, it may mean a promotion for him and he feels it is long overdue. "I need the money," he declares out loud while reaching for the lamp switch on his nightstand.

# CHAPTER 20

# GIFTED

At Meadowland Middle School, history is in the making. Never before has a 7th grader been accepted into the school Chorus until now. Generally speaking, this position has been reserved only for 8th graders. However, Kashonda has just received this prestigious honor and can't wait to share the good news with family and friends.

Her voice gleefully follows the notes performed on the finely tuned instrument played by Mrs. Tina Gladys, the Chorus music director. Kashonda's voice effortlessly flows from the highest to the lowest notes to the delight of all in listening range. Before the auditions, few were even remotely aware of the gifted voice Kashonda possesses. A sense of pride swells up in all who are privileged enough to be called her friend.

"Kashonda, I must say I am pleasantly surprised by your ability…Your gift…Your range," Mrs. Gladys exults while gliding her petite girly frame towards her. "I'm sure you can tell by the applause and my comments that you are accepted, my dear."

Mrs. Gladys has been so disappointed by previous students who quit up-stream that she has become hesitant about expressing any emotions at all towards her students.

"You're kidding! I don't believe it!" Kashonda yells while leaping and prancing around the room.

"I'm really in the chorus, right now? Woo-ooh!" she shouts. "Is this official?"

"We had no idea you had a voice like this," professes Linda Prowess, the assistant Chorus director. "Good luck!" she tells Kashonda while squeezing one hand and vigorously shaking the other. "Not that you'll need it," she winks.

It is a bright and sunny Denver day. There is hardly a cloud in the sky, Kashonda notices while on her way home. "Perfect, just perfect, she thinks, as she climbs down off of the school bus. Kashonda is anxious to tell family and friends all about the great day at school. Officially being accepted into the high school Chorus is a big deal and she wants the whole world to know.

"Hello!" she calls out while walking past the living room into the kitchen. "Is anybody here?" Apparently no one is home, so, Kashonda grabs an ice cream bar from the fridge and takes it to her room.

"I'm so excited I could scream, but, I won't!" she tells herself. "I'll dance!" she declares and sprints into a toe-pointed pirouette. She twirls, then curls before leaping into the air.

"I'm in the chorus," she shouts and throws herself onto the full-size bed. "I'm in the chorus," she sings in an operatic voice, then, rolls onto her back while kicking her feet into the air. "Me...Kashonda Leonard...Is in the chorus!" she yells at the top of her lungs. She leaps back down to the floor and twists to the beat of an imaginary drummer. Her movements become wild...unrestrained...free-style and even erratic. Until her precious collection of dolls are knocked onto the floor.

"Oh no, what have I done to my little darlings," she says while gently clutching them to her bosom.

A soft knock at the door brings her celebration to an end. Without hesitation, she positions the dolls back on top of the dresser and races to the door.

"Yes," she breathlessly answers. "Who is it?" The knob slowly turns.

"It's your Dad...Is it safe to come in?"

# CHAPTER 21

# NOT JUST A DOLL

As far as Kashonda is concerned, the typical dad would be home every night to tuck her into bed. He should, at least, be around to yell, "Do your homework!" Well, the man standing on the other side of the door is not your typical dad. Her father, Terrance Leonard, is an Airline Pilot and is seldom at home. Kashonda and her mother, Sharon Leonard, receive phone calls from all over the world, so, the few times he does come home are precious moments. He and Sharon enjoy spending time with one another and going club hopping. Before Kashonda's grandmother came into the picture, they sneaked her into the clubs with them. When Matilda got wind of it, she was appalled, so much so, that she packed her bags and showed up on their doorstep one day unannounced. She has lived with them ever since. That was 5 years ago and Kashonda is deeply grateful to her Grandmother for giving up her life for hers. Had it not been for her Matilda, she realizes, she never would have become a part of the church choir. Becoming a part of such a supportive group has given her the courage to participate in the school chorus.

Terrance cautiously enters his daughter's bedroom while counting the days since he was last home. They use to be as close as two peas-in-a-pod. Now, to his disappointment, the job takes precedents over everything, even his family.

"What happened here?" he wonders aloud while stepping over the few stuffed animals still laying on the floor.

"Oh these," she casually says so as not to cause alarm. "I bumped into them…That's all."

His inquisitive eyes look right through her like he knows her every thought.

"Oh– so that explains the noise we heard coming from this room?" he grins.

"I was dancing too," she explains while stumbling over her words. "I turned around and everything just fell," she smiles. "Happy now," she sasses.

"Just asking," he tells her with both hands raised defensively in the air.

The look in her restless eyes makes him acutely aware of how distant she has become. She misses him…This, he is certain of…And he misses her more than he thought he ever could. There was a time when he and Sharon actually did things together with their little girl. Watching her fidget around the room with her stuffed animals and dolls, forces him to admit that she's not their little girl any longer. The moment she was born, she became the center of their lives. However, all of that attention came to an abrupt end the moment he stepped into his new pilot position. Had he known becoming a pilot would come at such a high price, he would've chosen another profession.

"Something wonderful happened to me today," she tells him as he nonchalantly scans her room. "Aren't you going to asks me what?" she demands.

"Yes honey– What?" he wonders with a smile that is as warm as sunshine to his daughter.

"I was accepted into the chorus at school!" she beams.

His disinterests and pretenses of a smile have deeply wounded her in the past. Today, however, she sees a real heart-warming flicker in his eyes. Her Mom always says his job keeps him too preoccupied to be concerned with the little things at home. She hoped she was not considered to be a little thing to him. Even so, she has taken her mother's words to heart and stopped opening up to him, until now. Kashonda wants the whole wide world to know about this hidden treasure she possesses–especially her Dad.

"That sounds great baby!" a strong hand sandwiches her cheeks. "I'm really proud of you," he congratulates through a snug bear hug.

"Will you be..?" she begins to ask a question until he interrupts her with a kiss on the forehead.

"Got to go sweetheart…My flight leaves in one hour. You stay sweet and watch over your grandma and mother while I'm gone," he instructs while tilting his hand in a wave, then, rushing out of the room.

"There he goes again," she moans while sinking down into the purple and pink quilted comforter on her bed. Her sulking is momentarily interrupted by another faint knock at the door.

"Come in," she responds while clearing her throat.

"I almost forgot…Try not to knock anything over while I'm gone," he teases, then, gives her another kiss on the forehead.

After he leaves, she runs to the window overlooking the garage to watch her Dad back his silver Mercedes out of the driveway.

"I only wish he could come and hear me sing," she whines while propping Barbie against the dresser mirror. "He always cuts me off when I have an important question to ask," she pouts, then, rummages through the displayed dolls in search of G. W. Carver. "Now where is your new friend hiding Barbie?" she wonders. G. W. Carver looks on from the closet halfway expecting Barbie to answer. She gets down on one knee and searches under the bed for him. Then, she crawls to the nearby closet and scours the surrounding floor. Finally, she finds him in one of her, many, tissue-filled shoe boxes.

"There you are," she declares. "How in the world did you find your way over here?" she raises his body to eye level and studies his curiously wandering eyes.

"It's a good thing I did," he snaps. "You could have killed me," he harshly scolds.

Instantly, she drops the talking doll like a prickly vine, then, scrambles to her feet. Wobbly legs carry her down the stairs to the kitchen. There, she wonders whether she closed the bedroom door or not since the doll has come across as crazed and maniacal as "Chucky", the criminal possessed doll on the big screen. Tonight is not the time to be at home alone, she tells herself as a cold chill runs up her spine.

Being home alone has always been a big treat for Kashonda. It gives her the one opportunity to sing, laugh, and dance for as long and as hard as she pleases, without interruption. Now, she longs for a family member, any family member, to come in through the door and wake her out of this nightmare.

"Calm yourself," she consoles herself while reaching for a glass from the cabinet.

"Water!" she proclaims. "I'll have a drink of water. It's always soothing and helps me to think better too. That little demon is not going to defeat me!" Kashonda marches back upstairs to her room welding the kitchen broom and a screwdriver.

"Can this really be happening?" she wonders aloud. "Did that little man…doll…creature…really speak to me?"

The familiar squeak of the top step alerts G. W. Carver to her return. He has made up his mind to tell her the truth in hopes that she will assist him in returning to his associates. He feels as though this is the only way for him to get out of the menagerie he's a prisoner in now. In her absence, G. W. Carver climbs back onto the dresser and perches himself against her favorite stuffed animal, which is the pink bunny rabbit with over-sized white floppy ears.

Upon entering the room, she finds him seated among her stuffed animals and dolls with legs crossed and eyes fixed on her. His smile is menacing to say the least. Kashonda tosses the screwdriver she armed herself with to the floor and slowly approaches the dresser.

"You're real…Aren't you little man?" she asks while bending forward to get a closer look at him.

"Brilliant!" he mocks. "What a brilliant observation!" he scowls. G. W. Carver claps in a rhythmic one-two quarter beat.

"Stop it! Stop it!" she shouts while covering her ears. "It's not everyday that one of my dolls comes to life you know."

"Allow me to introduce myself," he entreats after regaining his composure. "I am known as G. W. Carver here on earth, an Ambassador from Troas, the third planet of the Quads Universe. While shopping for sustenance with my human liaison, a low-life took the bag I was in. He ran for a considerable distance before discarding me like trash and slinging me into a wall. My circuits went haywire and caused me to power down. You took me home with you, I assume, so here I am," he explains in one continuous breath.

"Incredible!" she exclaims. "Amazing!" she says while pacing back and forth. "I believe you! What should I do? Do I take you back to where I found you?" she questions with the utmost of sincerity in her voice. "I mean…" she pauses. "…Someone must be looking for you this very moment–Right?"

"Well, of course they are," he becomes indignant while searching for self-assuring words. "They will find me, so–we don't need to go back to that building. That terrible human may come back there looking for the bag that didn't belong to him in the first place," he snarls.

Kashonda wonders again if this moment is real, so, she pinches her arm, then, reaches for his as well. He darts out of her reach just in time to dodge her hand.

"What are you doing?" he belches.

"Oh, this is so exciting!" she prances around the room, then, reaches for the camera on top of the white dresser. "Can I take your picture? Wait until I tell Liz…Dorothy…Cheryl…" she babbles on and on until G. W. Carver abruptly cuts her off.

"You mustn't tell anyone about me!" he nervously shouts. "No one must know! I only let you know because it's time for me to have sustenance," he quickly explains.

"You mean food?" she wonders.

"Yes," he tells her, "Food."

# CHAPTER 22

# ALL FOR LAURA

Tom takes great pride in playing a critical role in his boss, Shakeam Evan's, success. This presentation today can make or break both of their chances for a promotion. So, he goes over the report he has compiled for the rising star of the office. Shakeam is vying to become the newest partner at Buffy, Taylor, and Turner law firm. However, long before becoming his paralegal assistant, Tom helped Shakeam become familiar with the politics of the firm. They've been best friends ever since.

The executive boardroom is behind Nancy's desk and no one enters without her permission. She is the executive secretary for all of the partners and all potential partner candidates must wait at her work station before their interviews. Shakeam looks like he is about to wear a hole in the olive green carpet. The faded and frayed carpet in front of Nancy's desk is evidence that many others have treadled this very same mountain before him. "Relax...," Tom encourages moments before Nancy buzzes Shakeam into the boardroom.

Tom goes back to his cubicle and along the way passes by a messenger who drops another work order into his in-basket. Burying himself into his work, he doesn't notice that it is already an hour past his lunchtime.

"Hey...Working through lunch today?" asks Laura. Her perfume fills the air like a refreshing soft breeze. It causes him to forget all about work... Shakeam...and the Visitors. He and Laura have worked together for 3 years and he has loved her for 3 years as well. She considers Tom to be her best friend. He wants her to be so much more. Laura nonchalantly rests a hand on his shoulder. She doesn't realize the jolt of excitement it gives him. He never lets on.

"Don't worry," she softly encourages. "He's a shoe-in," she assures him about Shakeam.

Tom leans back in his chair and studies her angelic face.

"Don't take it out on your computer," she jokes. She's careful not to let him know how much she loves his blushing smile.

"Oh! Yeah. Right," he hesitates while removing his hands from the keyboard.

"Okay, I didn't intend to interrupt your train of thought. Just thought I would break up the monotony. Got to go," she smiles.

His eyes follow her waltzing down the long narrow aisle. "Stupid! Stupid! Stupid!" he chides himself while hitting his forehead with the palm of a hand. "I should've told her how I feel about her. I felt something from her too. I know I did." He shakes his head from side to side. Previous attempts to reveal his feelings for Laura have all gone unnoticed. I do all a man can possibly do, he thinks, to let a woman know my true feelings. I send her good morning e-mails. I go out of my way to open doors for her. I buy gifts for her birthday. Flowers and candy on Valentine's Day. And, whenever she has a problem, my shoulder is always available for her to cry on. "What more can a man do," he says aloud while banging a hand down on his desk. Tom wonders whether he should conclude that she's as self-centered as the other women he works with. No! She couldn't possibly be that shallow. Could it be the only difference between her and them is his love? He sighs, resigning to the fact that he is hopelessly in love. Tom believes the office singles mostly go for the lawyers or partners and the next budding lawyer to be put on the auction block is, none other than, Shakeam.

Later that afternoon, Tom hears laughter spilling out of the boardroom along with its occupants. The sober expression on Shakeam's face does not reveal the immediate outcome of the meeting. Tom quickly swoops up a notepad and follows him into his office. Shakeam loosen his silk tie and hangs his Armani suit jacket on the back of a dark chocolate leather desk chair. His cool and calm demeanor is the same as it always is. Tom doesn't notice any tale-tale signs of defeat or success. Shakeam opens a bottle of spring water taken out of his mini-fridge and takes a long swig.

"I'm glad that's over," he says, then, wipes his mouth with the back of his hand.

"Oh?" Tom waits to here the news, good or bad.

"They drilled me without showing any signs of mercy," he tells Tom without hesitation. "I've got to give it to you, my friend. You did your homework. They tried to back me into a corner, but, your digging brought me out. If anybody deserves a raise, it is you my friend," he compliments while making a saluting gesture with his water bottle.

"Wait a minute..." Tom anxiously pleads. "Did you get it? Are you a partner now?"

Shakeam confidently smiles. "They'll let me know by the end of this week," he explains. "But it looks hopeful, very hopeful my friend," he confidently assures while taking another long swig of water.

# CHAPTER 23

# ELEVATOR TO ROMANCE

Cally read somewhere that the square enclosure in front of her is a transporter–of sorts. She's not sure that the word above it, *Elevator*, is an accurate description though. It has failed to elevate her and has not responded to her commands. "Take me to floor 12," she calmly demands for the fourth time. After several more unsuccessful attempts, a sharply dressed middle-aged woman enters the enclosure and graciously presses a numbered button on the wall. Cally is elated when the Elevator begins to move upward. It gradually slows to a stop, causing her to look up at the smooth panel above the door. The number 6 lights up in red above the Elevator door and the woman steps out into an empty hallway. Cally grins while pushing the button for 12.

In spite of Tom's explicit instructions for all of his visitors to remain indoors whenever he's not around, she has decided to strike out on her own. Tom is not expecting her to visit him on-the-job, even so, she's tired of being cooped-up in that one bedroom apartment with Frank and Terry all day, every day. They're sleep, she concludes, and I'm here to experience this new world.

Stepping off the elevator onto the right floor is easy enough, she thinks while allowing her keen senses to lead the way. She only knows the floor he works on, not the suite address. She takes wide strides down the first corridor. Then, when it comes to an end she makes a quick turn to the right. The hallway leads her to a huge open atrium where adjoining corridors extend in every direction. She passes men and women who stare her way, yet, offer no assistance. She senses Tom is nearby and walks faster to reach her destination. Finally, she reaches his office. Cally doesn't hesitate to approach a matronly woman sitting behind a desk enclosed in glass. Behind the woman is a wall with a large cutout window.

"I'm here to see Tom. I mean Tom Clancey," Cally sheepishly request.

Laura just so happens to be passing by the reception area when she hears a woman asking for her friend, Tom. Curiosity gets the best of her, so she ditches her paperwork onto a nearby desk and detours to meet this mild-mannered and stunningly attractive woman. Laura barges into the reception area and introduces herself before Nancy, the receptionist, has a chance to respond.

"Hi, I'm Laura. Tom is in a meeting. May I help you with something?" she politely inquires and gives her a quick glance from head-to-toe. "It looks like Tom has been holding out on me."

"Excuse me?" wonders Cally.

"Oh, don't mind me," Laura tells her with a pleasant smile. "I was just thinking out loud."

Cally returns the sweet smile and extends a hand just as she was taught to do by the Council. Laura returns a firm hand shake and wonders why Tom kept this honey-brown beauty out of their conversations.

"Well, I believe Tom will want to see me right away," insists Cally who is so resolute about it, Laura agrees without giving it another thought. She finds herself inexplicably knocking at Shakeam's door. She detests interrupting their meetings, just the same, she believes Tom wouldn't appreciate having a guest of his waiting in the lobby.

"Excuse me," Laura calls from the other side of the door.

"Come in!" Shakeam tells her.

Tom wonders what could be so important and Shakeam frowns while wondering the same thing.

"Excuse me…" her voice quivers. She feels tension rising in the room. "There's a Cally to see Tom. She's pretty persistent about it."

Tom jumps to his feet. "I'd better see what she wants!" he anxiously tells them before rushing out the door.

"I need to see this Cally for myself," says Shakeam who quickly blazes a trail behind him.

"You never mentioned her before," he snaps. "What's up with that?"

In the lobby, Cally has an all-about-the-weather chat with Nancy who politely offers her a seat. She respectfully declines and is all smiles when Tom enters the lobby.

"Ah…Hi!" he spits out while giving her a warm embrace. "What brings you here?" he wonders with suspicious eyes roaming over the sleek chocolate leather pants and matching vest. He bought this outfit for Cally on the day of her arrival. He thinks she looks great and way too good for this place. I know I'm responsible for the Visitors, he concludes, and this includes guarding her against the dangers of looking too good.

Shakeam is spellbound and envious of his friend's woman. He's never been speechless before, but, at this moment, he is at a loss for words. She is stunning, he tells himself while sizing her up with eyes full of lust. "Absolutely stunning," he says aloud while broadening a giddy smile.

"You can give me your reasons over lunch," Tom tells her then turns to Shakeam. "This is Cally, my cousin."

Shakeam waves Tom to the side, stepping in between him and the woman he believes he's been waiting for all of his life.

"Hello! I'm Shakeam," he pauses while slowly checking her out from head-to-toe. "And your name is?" he asks in a low sensuous tone.

He's not like Tom at all, she notices. And he's so much taller and stands erect like the warriors on planet Mistique. I'd like to get to know this human a little better, maybe a lot better, she concludes.

"I'm known as Cally here on earth," she absentmindedly replies through a blush.

He extends his hand for her to shake, then, crowns it with the other one. He allows it to rest on top of hers for a brief moment. Then, lifts her soft hand to his mouth and gently brushes his lips against it.

The instant attraction is so apparent, Tom fears he has to do something and do it quickly. So, for lack of a better plan, he jumps between them.

"Cally is not from here," he nervously points out. "She shouldn't be here," he stammers. "I mean…"

Shakeam nudges him out of the way again and nestles her arm beneath his. "We're going to lunch. You coming?" he asks Tom in a tone that sounds more like a command.

"Of course," Tom gulps while wondering how he will ever explain the true identity of Cally to his boss and best friend.

Why did she choose that body? Of all the bodies in the world to choose from, she uses one most men are attracted to. Tom makes a mental note to question her later about the way she looked at Shakeam with those beautiful brown eyes. The question in his mind is whether her species is capable of falling in love and copulating with a human.

Walking a few blocks down the street to Houston's, their favorite lunch spot, only takes about 5 minutes. Apparently, its a favorite for a host of others as well. It's buzzing with people waiting in the overflow and lined up on the sidewalk leading to the street. "Lucky for us, I made reservations on our way over," he brags while grabbing Cally by the hand. "Follow me!" He works his way through the crowd until he reaches the reservations desk. Raul, the Maitre'd notices him and immediately clears and cleans the booth next to the front wall of windows.

All eyes follow the Maitre'd who escorts them to their seat. Tom suspects Shakeam must be paying him under the table. Even so, Tom is impressed by the way Shakeam got them into one of the best tables in the restaurant in less than 5 minutes. He always has to wait at least 45 minute before being seated.

Shakeam likes the fact that the view of the mountains is a good focal point and a great topic for starting a conversation. The window seat is Shakeam's favorite spot. Even so, he's considering asking for a more secluded table the next time he comes with her alone. He's already making plans to see her again.

"So, tell me," Shakeam stares. "How long have you and Tom been dating?"

"Oh, we're not dating," she quickly corrects. "We're just friends."

"Cousins," Tom reminds him while worrying that Shakeam is falling for an alien, head first.

"I'm disappointed," Shakeam sighs while searching for the right words. "No, I am hurt," he finally concludes.

Cally eases forward in her seat. She wants to hear every word this human has to say. Why is that? she wonders.

"Tom, my best friend, has a fine woman like you as a friend or cousin and he never bothers to even mention your name to me," he explains while kicking Tom's shins under the table. Tom moans while cutting his eyes at Cally. "Why is that Tom?" he teases.

"I couldn't," Tom stutters while reaching down to rub his bruised shin.

"I wasn't here before," she jumps in to save Tom from the embarrassment. Shifting eyes go from one person to the other as Cally examines their words as well as their hearts and finds them both to be sincere. "This is my first time visiting Denver," she explains. "Right Tom?"

Tom fumbles the ball and attempts to recover it by projecting more confidence. "Oh yes, that's right." He sounds self-assured now.

While sitting across from her, Shakeam is amazed by how much he longs to be with Cally. He never dreamed it could be possible. Even so, he believes he has found his soulmate. The two of them talk over their lunch, over their coffee and, then, over their dessert while ignoring constant interruptions from Tom. Shakeam suggests, more than once, that Tom return to the office without them. "I'll make sure to return her to you safely," Shakeam promises. After being totally aggravated, Tom reminds Shakeam of their responsibility to their place of employment in order to pry him away from the table.

"Well, we have to get back to the office now," Tom insists. "We're in the middle of a new project and all eyes have been on us. Getting back to the office is a must today of all days."

She is well-aware that Tom and Shakeam have work waiting on them at the office. For some reason unknown to her, she is not interested in following protocol or their work hours. She simply wants to continue her conversation with this interesting man she just met. Shakeam's words are alive and vibrant, while Tom's words have suddenly become annoying echoes in her head.

"Cally, I never knew you could be so shallow," Tom goads while observing her school-girl-crush behavior.

This gives her time to absorb all of the words of this man and delve a little deeper inside his head.

Shakeam examines her hair, strand-by-strand, and romanticizes about how wonderful it would look in his hands. Her faun-like nose and voluptuous lips entice him far beyond words can describe. I've only known her for an hour, he thinks, even so, it feels like I want to be with her forever.

Cally is baffled by this strong emotion stirring inside of her belly. When it comes to this particular human, she finds herself noticing the cinnamon spice tint of his skin and is keenly aware of the strength in his hands. His touch is warm and gives her an unfamiliar sensation. She has come to the conclusion that this human is so much more real than any shape shifter could ever hope to be. She sees herself though as an impostor. In spite of Tom's objections, Cally decides to explore all of the in's and out's of human behavior. She is determined to find out why Shakeam is so attracted to her and why she is so taken-back with him.

Tom waves a hand between them to get their attention one more time.

"It's time to go," he pleads in frustration.

Without warning, he whistles, causing the entire restaurant to perk up and take notice.

"We're coming," resigns Shakeam, displaying a tick of annoyance with Tom. "No more whistling, my friend," he sighs.

# CHAPTER 24

# POPCORN BREAK

A sudden gust of wind lifts leaves high into the air just as Cally picks up the fresh scent of G. W. Carver. With the wave of a hand, she summons Frank and Terry to follow her away from the empty parking lot of the church.

Her present form provides little protection against the Arctic night air. So, she takes on a new form and the black jaguar she chooses suits her well. It also provides ample protection against below freezing temperatures. The agile new frame purrs and rubs against Frank's leg for a moment. A nudge from her nose signals him to continue moving straight ahead. "Who does she think she is," Terry mumbles from behind. She speeds up, passes Cally, then, snaps her nose up towards the air for the jaguar to see. Cally ignores Terry and stretches her stride while occasionally releasing a deep throaty purr. The faster pace forces Frank and Terry to skip, hop, and occasionally flutter their wings in order to keep up.

They round a corner and straightway enter an area bustling with people. So, while no one is looking, Cally conceals herself in a nearby alley while reverting back to human form.

The other streets they've travelled on were practically deserted. In contrast, this street has bright neon signs flashing in various shop windows. They notice all sorts of cars and SUVs slowly cruising down the well-lit streets. Some cars bounce while others spin their expensive rims. Some vehicles are deliberately holding up traffic by stopping where there are clearly no stop lights. And Cally is particularly puzzled by the fact that women on street corners out in this cold are not bundled up for the weather. She concludes that the fashions made for women of this world are for aesthetic purposes only.

Frank and Terry decide to do a little studying of their own and drift towards a human sitting in a glass enclosed booth. The booth sits in front of a building marked "Theatre". Terry gravitates towards the booth while Frank follows his nose towards the smell of food.

"Hello! How are you?" Terry cheerfully greets the man sitting in the booth. "Could you tell me your purpose in this glass enclosure?"

At first, the ticket clerk is puzzled by her crude features illuminated by the bright theater lights.

"Oh, I get it," he sighs. "You were sent over here by Scott, weren't you?" he assumes. Terry is intrigued by his thick Hispanic accent and sly grin.

She shrugs her shoulders and stares at him with a blank expression. He is not able to determine her character role and takes great pride in always being right on-the-money. For a moment, he believes her costume is the real McCoy, meaning, it doesn't look like a costume at all.

"Well, you tell him it's not Halloween yet," he snickers and mumbles something in Spanish.

Terry laughs with him though baffled by his comment.

"To answer your question," he muses while slowly chanting each word. "I-am-here-to-sell-tickets for the movies. Would you like to buy one?" He points to the movie selection board on the wall behind him.

Cally enters the large lobby and watches Terry stare at the large framed posters on the walls.

"Buy what?" Cally demands while pushing Terry aside with the swoop of a hand.

The ticket clerk smiles down at her while scanning as much of her body as he can from the booth. "Are you with her?" She senses the increase in his pulse rate.

"Yes," Cally impatiently responds and is seriously considering eliminating him on the grounds of dislike. "Is everything okay?" she demands of the attendant who keeps leaning towards the window to get a closer look at her hourglass figure.

"This is sweet. Too—too sweet," he says in a slow high pitch drawl. "Did Scott just send you over here too? I'll be off in an hour baby…Wait for me," he demands with a wink and this time his smile reveals a shimmering gold front tooth.

She categorically denies knowing anyone named Scott and informs him she is searching for someone who disappeared behind the booth.

"Terry…Where's Frank?" she ask in a panic.

Terry shrugs her shoulders as Cally's demeanor changes from pleasant to fearful.

"You clowns need to move out of the way," orders the ticket clerk. "I got customers lining up.

Cally grabs Terry by the collar and pulls her to the side.

"We have to find Frank!" she says through clinched teeth.

Terry's nonchalant attitude makes Cally even angrier.

"Did you hear? Don't you understand? Frank is missing!" she over-stresses. "We don't know where he is."

"Don't worry," Terry says in a comforting manner. "Wherever there is food, that's where he will be," she sighs and sniffs the air around them. "That way!" she points with confidence towards the source of the aroma. Her nose carries her towards it and Cally follows close behind. They cautiously elude the eyes of the ticket clerk who would rightfully demand payment.

Inside the theater, a large crowd is gathered in the well-lit lobby. The smell of food is captivating, even to Cally, yet, there is still no sign of Frank. Both of their eyes are drawn to the life-size posters lining the walls. The posters are depictions of vessels traveling through space.

"Oh, I see you two are Trekkers," one man observes from behind.

They both informally turn towards the direction of the voice.

"Trekkers…?" Cally wonders.

"Well, you know," the man points a finger towards the sky. "You guys like sci-fi? That Star Wars movie is in there now."

The ladies exchange glances after admiring his black one-piece spandex suit with a thick gold belt. It reminds Cally of the suits the navigators wear while transporting passengers to and from planets. They both wonder whether he could be a star traveler or not?

"We're looking for one of our friends," Cally explains after taking a deep breath. "He would be dressed like her." She points to Terry who is now facing the direction of the lobby. He closely examines what he believes to be, Terry's costume. The man is intrigued by her life-like lizard features. He pulls back her robe and is amazed by the intricate details of her costume and seamless mask.

"Far out!" he exclaims with a tremendous amount of admiration. "I've been trekking for more than 20 years and I've never seen a costume quite like this one before. Where's the party?"

Cally's impatience begins to show. "There is no party. We simply need to locate our friend."

"Ouch!" he exclaims and rebounds to Terry. "This is just for you pretty lady," he winks at Terry, then, hands her his card. "It's going to be a big Halloween bash this year. And right now, you and your friend swimming in the popcorn over there will win 1st prize–hands-down."

An arm slips around Terry's thick waist and slowly turns her in the direction of Frank who is inside the tank of popcorn.

"You may want to hurry about getting your friend out of their. The police will be here soon," he warns. "And make sure you bring some of whatever he's on to the party," he winks again before disappearing into a theater room.

Cally overhears their conversation and stampedes her way through the crowd to the concession stand where Frank is the main attraction. The crowd laughs and cheers at Frank on the other side of the counter. He's eating popcorn as fast as the spinning carousel can spit it out. Totally oblivious to the roaring crowd, he turns around long enough to catch a glimpse of Cally and Terry.

"Uh—oh!" he says while turning to face them with an overstuffed mouth full of popcorn. "It's good! I mean really great!" he shouts over the melee around them. "You two should try some," he offers while stretching two popcorn-filled hands towards them.

# CHAPTER 25

# ARACHNOPHOBIA

On the other side of town, G. W. Carver faces more challenges at his captor's lair.

He is left perched on top of her antique white dresser, presumably for his safety. Being kept next to stuffed animals and life-like dolls is not his idea of exploring. He runs a hand down the hair of the mulatto Princess Barbie doll and wishes she were real. At least I'd have someone my size to talk with, he thinks. "I am becoming stir-crazy!" he shouts while throwing up his hands. These emotions are totally new to him and not very easy to digest. He comes to the conclusion that it must be the earth's atmosphere changing his molecular makeup. A tear rolls down one cheek and a trembling hand wipes it away. "Get a hold of yourself...You jerk!" he shouts, then, decides there is only one solution to this melancholy–he must find a way to escape.

With teary hope-filled eyes, he makes his way down the 3-drawer dresser to the floor. His legs carry him over to the chest located at the foot of his abductor's bed. On top of it rests the book he has been so enthralled about. "B-I-B-L-E," he slowly spells the gold engraved title of the book. He reads up to the book of Psalms, meditates on all it says, then, continues until he finishes the entire Bible. G. W. Carver records the red passages and makes assessments of the meanings. "Peace on earth...Good will towards men," he reads. "Interesting concept," he concludes while pondering the meaning of it all.

"Ah!" he says after seeing a laptop computer on the other side of the room. He does a flip onto the floor and nails a perfect 10 landing.

"Perfect," he applauds himself while heading towards the desk in the far corner of the spacious room. "Are my associates making progress at evaluating these humans?" he wonders. So far, he finds them to be thoroughly detestable. There is crime reported daily in nearly every neighborhood and he notices that most of this crime is against the human body. There are shootings, murders, robberies, rapes and a multitude of unethical acts committed daily on planet Earth. The rest of the universe considers these infractions to be acts against the natural order of Society. Of course, he concludes, if peace on earth, as it says in the bible, is really wanted, maybe they'll survive in the end.

The patter of footsteps draws attention away from his thoughts. G. W. Carver glances over his right shoulder. "It's nothing," he sighs and reasons if it is someone or something there, surely they will make themselves known. Every time he takes a step forward he hears someone or something trailing close behind.

"Almost there," he tells himself.

The gap between the dresser and the desk is not far for a person of average stature. However, for someone only 12 inches tall it is a measurable distance.

He casually lifts a leg to climb up to the desk, when, suddenly a force tosses him down to the floor. This thing lassos him with a sticky rope-like substance. Then, it swiftly pulls him away from the desk. G. W. Carver flips his body around to see the source of the attack. It is a creature unknown to him. Its black furry legs race to reel him closer towards impending doom. G. W. Carver cringes at the two black fangs positioned on either side of its mouth. With lightening speed he scrambles to his feet with the rope-like substance still wrapped around his neck.

"You think you can eat me!" he yells at the eight legged creature. "I'll kill you and serve you for dinner!" he shouts while pulling it to the floor with the strength of its own rope. He flips it to its side and, using the rope, ties all eight legs together. "That'll teach you," he sneers, then, swipes his hands together at record speed to rid them of the sticky residue of the spider's rope.

G. W. Carver leaves the creature to continue his quest to the top of the desk.

"Yes! Yes! I made it," he cheers, then quickly turns his attention to the computer.

"On!" he commands the computer while expecting it to speedily obey.

After a few more commands fail to render a response, he resorts to pushing every button and key until it finally comes on.

"I knew I could do it!" he proudly proclaims with arms raised in a victorious V. "Now let me see if I can figure out how it works," he stares at the screen. "I think I'll look up eight-legged furry creatures first."

# CHAPTER 26

# G. W. CARVER SHORT-CIRCUITS

The dial of the lock spins to the left, then, Kashonda turns it to the right. It should've opened by now, she pouts.

"What's wrong with you girl?" asks Liz, her best friend whom she has known since the first grade. "You've been sulking from one class to the next all day long," Liz gets in her face. "Oh yeah, I noticed. Uh hum…Just didn't say anything until now. I would think that with all of the good things happening to you lately, you'd be walking on air right about now," she laughs.

Kashonda shrugs her shoulders and mumbles. "I know you're right girl."

Liz leans against the next locker and keeps a close eye on her friend. "Don't tell me you forgot your combination. We're in the middle of the school year. Write it on your hands like I do."

She knows her friend has good intentions, however, Liz's persuasive argument has no power over her, not today anyway. The situation at-hand is more powerful than anything she ever could've imagined. Not being able to share G. W. Carver's true identity with anyone has her on edge. The notion of inadvertently becoming host to a 12-inch creature from another world is mind-boggling. G. W. Carver has taken center-stage in her life now, and, as far as she's concerned, all attention should be on him. Her insides ache to tell her best friend. Sharing this monumental episode of her life with someone is all she desires to do. And now, due to a promise, she can't share the most fantastic discovery of her life with anyone, not even her closest friend. Her most amazing discovery must remain a secret.

"Kashonda," Liz calls. "Hello, earth-to-Kashonda. We're having a talk here."

The slamming of the locker door startles her out of the stupor, but, only for a second.

"Sorry…I didn't mean to be rude," Kashonda apologizes while gracefully easing away. "I'll talk with you later. Okay?"

Liz watches her friend race down the hall until she is out of sight. She wonders why Kashonda shut her out for the very first time since they've known each other. Liz doesn't want to let this go unchallenged. So, she vows to find out what's bothering her if that's the last thing she does in her young life.

On Kashonda's way to chorus, she is thankful and hopeful that this class will help her forget about talking dolls, absent fathers and anything else that bothers her. This is a new class, a tremendous honor and she intends to savor every moment.

Suddenly, the pressure of being on display frightens her. So, she slips into the first seat available. At the moment, she wants to be just another member of the group rather than a trophy.

"Hello Miss Kashonda…We have pre-assigned seats according to our voice pitch," the instructor explains. "You're Alto, so, you belong on that second seat in the second row," she leads the way with a quick wave of the hand.

"Since this is Kashonda's first day…I expect everyone to make her feel at home."

While the teacher holds out a welcome package, Kashonda starts to feel awkward again and sinks down in her chair.

"The music students immediately gather around her with hand shakes, hugs, and hardy pats on the back. She's overwhelmed by their kindness and momentarily forgets about her alien friend perched on top of the dresser in her bedroom.

During class, her singing gift flows like melting butter and the nightingale voice reaches triumphant peaks which spawn lengthy applauds and cheers from her instructor as well as from peers. Her gift has made room for her and for this she is deeply grateful to God.

Meanwhile, in no time at all, G. W. Carver masters the central operations of Kashonda's computer. He waltzes across the keyboard to spell out the topics of interest.

"Ah, here it is. Arachnophobia," he reads. "The fear of spiders…And spiders…Here we are."

His search leads him to a creature resembling the one he hog-tide.

"Here it is. Furry! Black! Red dot! Poisonous! They have been known to kill their victims!"

He shivers at the thought of being bitten by such a venomous creature. An unexplainable amount of fear surges from within and short-circuits his system. His body stiffens. It falls backwards onto the keyboard and flips over. Then, it slides down, head-over-heels, onto the desk. G. W. Carver has blacked-out again. Only this time his black out is from raw fear.

# CHAPTER 27

# SECRET LOVE

Tom stumbles over the elevator threshold before glancing at his watch. It is 7 a.m. and he knows he needs to be sharper than this in order to persuade Shakeam to give him time off during the busy season. Tom is counting on Shakeam appreciating the fact that he has come in an hour early each day for two weeks to clear his work load. The last time he took off, Tom had to hire a fill-in. He knows Shakeam won't go it alone, not even for one day, and he's asking for at least three. Tom has decided to tell him it's a family illness and that he's needed right away. And then, Tom will volunteer to work late to finish the projects he's been working on for the past two weeks. This is the way Tom hopes the conversation will go.

The elevator does its usual jerk before coming to a complete stop at Tom's floor. The moment he steps onto the floor he notices the receptionist is missing. "Bogo!" Tom shouts aloud. She is known for her gift of gab. He whizzes past the empty desk with Laura's gift in hand.

"These pink carnations should do the trick," he says aloud. "Laura once told me that her ideal man would bring her a dozen pink carnations for no special reason at all."

Tom carefully places the flowers in a vase and meticulously arranges them just the way they appeared in the florist window. He writes: FROM SOMEONE WHO CARES ESPECIALLY FOR YOU.

The morning is still early, so there is no chance of Laura, or her spying friends, sneaking up on him.

An hour later, Laura pulls into the company parking garage and while looking up into the sky, she smiles at the sight of the sun casting a silver lining around a cluster of gray clouds. "Today is my lucky day," she tells herself. Moments later, she pulls into her favorite parking spot. While walking across the catwalk, she assures herself that good fortune is waiting to kiss her. Anxious to beat the clock, she makes a b-line for her cubicle chair and nearly topples over a vase of flowers at her desk. A card falls out from the bouquet and she stretches to grab it before it hits the floor.

"Now, who could've known that pink carnations are my favorite flower," she wonders while pulling the card out of the envelope.

Around the corner Tom listens and notices she is pleased with the surprise. This gives him a warm glow of hope.

"FROM SOMEONE WHO CARES ESPECIALLY FOR YOU," she reads aloud.

"Ooh…This is so sweet…I could cry," she swoons while kissing the tiny card.

"Shakeam," she whispers. "It must be him."

No one hears Laura, not even Tom who is standing behind her.

"Ah—um," Tom clears his throat.

Disappointed by the intrusion, she swirls around to see who it is.

"Oh! You startled me. How long have you been standing there?"

"Long enough to see you admire your flowers," he replies with a wide grin.

"Aren't they beautiful?" She touches the tips while drawing the bouquet towards her. The mildly sweet fragrance tickles her nose.

"They smell wonderful! I love them," she adds. "As a matter of fact, they're just like the ones I described to you. I know someone must have told him. You know: my-knight-in-shining-armor. Was it you?" she muses without expecting him to confess. "Of course," she teases. "You're the only one who knew, but then, you could have spilled the beans to someone else," she pauses.

The inference made is of Shakeam and Tom doesn't like it. Practically every woman in the office is stuck on a lawyer. So, he pouts, why should this one be any different? Her comment was like a dagger penetrating deep into his heart.

"Got to go," he excuses himself. He wants to get as far away from her as possible.

"Just like that?" she wonders.

"Ah…You know," he excuses while backing out of her cubicle. "There's always another meeting in this place."

Tom walks towards Shakeam's office, wondering whether they should remain best friends or become enemies. Laura is off limits, he thinks, and she always will be. The door is partially open, so, Tom barges in.

"Morning," he greets Shakeam while anxiously settling into the chair across from him.

"Is something bothering you?" Shakeam wants to know after noticing the stress lines creasing Tom's forehead. "You look worried my friend."

Tom leans back in the chair and sighs.

"I'll tell you later," he promises. "I came in here for now because of an emergency I have at home. I need to take a few days off this week," he nervously explains. Shakeam grants him his requested time off with ease. Even so, Tom can't seem to shake the uncertainty about developing a serious relationship with Laura.

"Is there anything else I can do for you?"

Tom's tense body relaxes the moment he pushes back in the soft leather captain-back chair across from Shakeam's desk.

"Well," he pauses. "There is one thing you can do for me."

Shakeam searches Tom's desperate blue eyes.

"Sure. Anything you need Buddy."

Tom nervously clears his throat. "This morning I brought Laura two dozens of her favorite flowers and she thinks..." he pauses. "She thinks you bought her the bouquet of carnations instead."

Shakeam leaps to his feet, enraged at the thought.

"What!" his voice is loud enough for the entire floor to hear. "Where did she get a dumb idea like that?" he demands.

Tom's weak legs manage to wobble into a stance.

"She's been confiding in me about having feelings for you," he explains.

"Yes, I heard. She's crazy about me isn't she?" Shakeam proudly pats himself on the chest a couple of times.

"Well," Tom clarifies. "I never told you...But I'm crazy about her!"

Shakeam's expression becomes sober.

"Laura? I always thought you two were just buddies," he tells him.

The room is suddenly quiet and Shakeam wonders what favor his friend will ask of him next. He's a little leery of being caught in the middle of a love triangle.

"If anyone asks about the flowers," he pauses. "Tell them they are from me. I want everyone to know. Maybe, once it gets back to her, she'll appreciate who they came from."

Shakeam exhales in agreement. "Oh, is that all," he sighs. "Anything for you, pal."

# CHAPTER 28

# PREPARATIONS

Cally prepares for her first date with a human. She knows they just met, nevertheless, she is convinced that this date is strictly for scientific purposes. On the other hand, Tom is not so sure. For this reason, he has begged and pleaded with her not to go on the date.

She looks forward to finding out how humans build relationships. Within the Nebula where she was born, the males and females only come together once a year. This is for the sole purpose of reproducing. On earth, she is amazed to discover that some couples stay together for years and never reproduce. She concludes that the body she's chosen is definitely attracted to this specific human. It's like an unseen force has climbed inside of her loins and is drawing them together. I need to know all of the ramifications of these human emotions. It has been documented that some individuals of her species do not have the ability to control their emotions. She now wonders whether she could be one of them.

The pasted grin on Tom's face just won't go away. He grins at all of the passengers on the train. He smiles at the people on the bus. Then, he is still smiling while slipping a key into the lock of his apartment. He is relieved that the Lizaradactiles are still asleep in the closet. But, not seeing Cally around really concerns him. He looks around the main living area, then, checks the other rooms. "What is going on?" he wonders out loud. "She should be here!" Suddenly his eyes are drawn to the note on the refrigerator. It reads: "Hi, I hope you'll understand. I'm on a date with Shakeam." The bowl in his hand topples onto the floor. He bangs a fist down onto the counter. "Now what am I suppose to do!" he says through clinched teeth. "I'll continue with what I'm doing," he says while browning chicken in an air fryer. "She's a big girl...woman, and she should be able to take care of herself." He boils a pot of water for the rice. "I'm done with her." He swipes his hands together and, then, puts all of his effort into cooking a meal fit for a king.

Tom doesn't need to wake the Lizaradactiles…The scent of the food is doing that already. The menu is as follows: four roasted chickens– gone within 10 minutes; six large burgers– gone within 8 minutes; two large gallon size trays filled with roasted potatoes– gone within 6 minutes; six pounds of deli ham also gone within 2 minutes. They're not partial to vegetables, but Tom decides to put together two large serving bowls of salad fixings as a filler. Frank and Terry's crude behavior is growing on him. He simply needs to remember to stay out of their feeding zone.

"If you two don't mind," he tells them while taking a whiff of his underarms. "I'm going to jump into the shower."

He gives them a thumbs-up and disappears into his bedroom.

Frank gives Terry a bewildered look. "What do we do now?" he wonders.

Terry jumps to her feet. "Oh! I know. I know!" she says while frantically waving a hand in the air.

"Spill it out Dodo bird," Her nervous ticks really irritate him, but, he likes every minute of it.

Tom dresses but is too distressed to clean the messy kitchen or even cook for himself.

"Did you two get enough to eat?" he wonders.

"We sure did," answers Terry.

"Speak for your self," Frank candidly responds. "I could use a little more." He picks up a dirty dish and hands it to Tom.

# CHAPTER 29

# THE SCOLDING

His body stiffens across the keys at the sound of approaching footsteps. "Oh G. W. Carver!" she scolds while inviting him into her hand. "How did you get way over here? I thought I told you to stay hidden on the dresser. Had someone else walked in they may have become suspicious. Everyone knows I'm too old to play with dolls," she explains and places him back on the dresser.

He couldn't argue with that, except, he doesn't know exactly how old she is. And he doesn't know whether playing with dolls at her age is appropriate or not.

"Before you say any more, I'll have you know that I don't take orders from humans, especially not from one who's not even fully grown yet. And for your information a Rumerangue would go crazy staring at a bunch of stuffed toys all day. And by-the-way, I needed something to read, so, I read your bible for the second time."

He leans to the side and rests one hand against her Barbie doll.

"Then, I wanted to search for more historical data. I noticed you on that machine looking up topics for your school report the other day, so, I decided to do the same. While on route to it, a spider attacks me. It could've killed me with one bite!" he gasps. "I looked up spiders and discovered this one is poisonous."

Kashonda cringes at the sight of it and recalls it is the same kind that bit her father in the toe last year. His foot was swollen twice its normal size for over a month. Then, he had to take antibiotics for at least two weeks to break his high fever. G. W. Carver surely would've died, she tells herself. And it probably would have eventually bitten her as well. So as not to alarm

G. W. Carver any further, she decides not to tell him about the scorpions roaming about too.

"Thank God, you killed it. My Dad was bitten by its mate 2 weeks ago. You know they always roam in pairs," she adds.

"No, I had no idea," he gulps. "We don't have those where I come from."

She scoops the spider up with a piece of notebook paper and carries it out of the room.

"I'll be right back," she promises. "Want something to eat when I come back?"

"Of course I do," he huffs. "Find me something green this time"

The door closes behind her. "I hope she heard me," he tells himself, then, plops down on the paw of a pink fluffy bunny.

"What a day! What could possibly be keeping my associates from rescuing me?" he wonders.

At the apartment, Frank relaxes in a lounge chair on the patio. The cool night air soothes his restless heart for the moment. He takes the time to gaze deep into the star-filled sky and allows his mind to carry him back to the night before. The smell of buttery popcorn filled his nostrils. Jeers from the crowd excited him. And the element of danger stirred his primal instincts. Now, he hungers to hunt for prey like the ones he had on his home planet. Frank envies Cally for stealing away to the movies. He imagines there will be popcorn there and lots of it.

"Poor, poor G. W. Carver," he says aloud. "He's the historian among us," he revels, "Yet, he's missing all of these incredible happenings. I must thank him when he's finally located, thinks Frank. Had it not been for him, I wouldn't even know what a theater is.

# CHAPTER 30

# CALLY'S DATE

The movie is almost over and Cally has yet to find one fascinating feature about it. Shakeam, on the other hand, appears to be in another dimension. His eyes are glued to the screen and, with one hand over hers, he gently squeezes every time bullets fly and his favorite actor dodges another flying fist. "Did you see that?" he continues to ask in amazement. By now, she has learned not to answer. The proper thing to do is simply ride the wave of excitement with him. She merely nods, smiles and wishes she could share the fact that defying gravity is commonplace where she's from. Anxious for the movie to end, she excuses herself by pretending she needs to visit the ladies room. He tells her she is leaving during the best part. Just the same, she nods, then, politely excuses her self. "I won't be long," she whispers.

The lobby looks like a safe place to wait and to focus her thoughts on the real purpose for being on Earth. We have to find G. W. Carver tonight, she tells herself. He has to be tired, hungry, and so, so alone. No one can help him because no one knows he is real. I must leave this place, she worries–I need to leave now.

Moments later, floods of chattering movie patrons pour into the lobby from the theater she came out of. Eager eyes scan the room for Shakeam. She's both relieved and panicked as she notices him working his way through the crowd to reach her. Shakeam doesn't bother to conceal his enthusiasm while fighting against the tides of people coming and going to get to her.

"That was a good movie. Sorry you missed the end. Are you all right? We'll have to come back to see it again," he promises all in one breath. "What were you doing out here for so long?" he wonders.

"Well, I was…" she attempts to explain until he cuts her off.

"Never mind…I know it must have been important. Is everything okay?" he asks again.

Outside, he gently slips his black leather jacket across her shoulders, then, seductively caresses her from behind. Cally has never been touched this way before and to her surprise, she finds it quite appealing.

"I feel like I'm needed at home," she explains with a sense of urgency in her voice.

He slips one hand into hers as they exit the theatre and surmises she must be needed at home for the same family emergency Tom mentioned earlier. Maybe taking her out tonight was wrong timing, he concludes. Something about her has intrigued him more than any woman of his past. This is why he has made up his mind not to let this woman go.

Cally fumbles with the key at the door when Shakeam startles her by pressing his body against her from behind. He gently turns her body towards his and causes their lips to touch. She gives in to their first kiss. Her body burns with desire for this man. His hormones rage even so he respects her body language. Her body stiffens as she softly pushes him away. She knows herself well enough to recognize all she must do while living on this strange planet. Had it not been for G. W. Carver going missing, she would surely explore this human intimacy even further.

She reaches for the apartment door, still trembling from the kiss. Her damp palms slide over the door knob, yet, she manages to turn it until it clicks open.

"How was your date?" Terry asks the moment Cally steps over the threshold. "I can't imagine how it must feel to be with a human." Terry blushes.

Frank pulls his mate to the side.

"I can't imagine you with a human either," he cracks.

"Nobody asked you," Terry sneers and grinds a pillow into his alarmed face.

"Cally We have to talk!" an angry Tom demands and pulls her by the arm into his bedroom.

"Sit down!" he orders.

She gracefully seats herself at the foot of the bed.

"My feet are killing me…" she sighs while pulling off a pair of stilettos. "Oh—excuse me," she apologizes for rubbing her feet in his presence.

"Shakeam is a man," he begins.

Cally looks perplexed. Of course, she knows he is the male of the species.

"I know you know this on the surface. But we men have certain appetites. And when we have a taste for something well, only the real thing will do. Understand?" he searches her childlike expression and hopes for an intelligible response.

"Well," he continues. "Shakeam really likes you and I don't want him to fall for someone he can't truly have. Understand?"

Cally nods in agreement, even though her eyes say otherwise.

"I understand. You don't want me to disappear one day, as you know I must, and leave him in this mental state of infatuation," she elaborates.

"Exactly," he solemnly agrees. "Now that we're thinking alike, I feel a lot better."

She motions him to the door with the wave of a hand. "I need to get ready now," she tells him. "Ready for what?" he wonders.

"We're going to find G. W. Carver tonight!" she resolves. Her demeanor says it all. Tom concludes it will be useless to try to dissuade her.

# CHAPTER 31

# THE RESCUE

The Aliens travel through downtown Denver again and retrace their steps from the night before. In spite of the burdensome restraints put on him by Cally, Frank longs to satisfy the yearnings of his hungry flesh.

"Don't even think about it," she warns after Frank presses his nose against a candy shop window.

"I was just looking," he defends and deeply inhales the scents of sweet dainties.

"Tonight is G. W. Carver's night and I don't want you spoiling it for him again," she sternly protests.

They enter a suburban community that holds an air of familiarity about it. Cally detects G. W. Carver's scent in the air all around them and she knows, beyond a shadow of a doubt, that he's nearby.

"The trail ends here," she sighs in front of a 2-story brick home with mauve shutters and door. "He is somewhere in this dwelling."

She jerks Frank by the collar just as he begins to sounds-off a ceremonial Lizaradactile howl.

"Let's not tell the whole world we're here just yet," she warns.

The open window above the patio looks inviting enough for her to climb through. So, she balances herself on the trash can beneath it and gives the window a swift push upward. First time around it refuses to budge, but, the second time works like a charm. Well, it works until her foot slips and knocks over the trash cans. Suddenly, the unwelcome clanging of the metal trash can sounds an alarm that is heard throughout the neighborhood. Dogs bark. Owls hoot. And backyard flood lights come on. Frank and Terry escape into nearby trees, leaving Cally to fend for her self. Staying focus and leaving the noise behind, she enters the residence. Unbeknownst to her, a silent alarm is triggered and the police are on their way.

Meanwhile, G. W. Carver rolls over while dreaming he'd just been rescued by his associates. It seems so real he sits straight up and is too restless to go back to sleep now. Suddenly, a beam of light shines through the bedroom window and causes Kashonda to sit up in bed too.

"What's going on?" she wonders through a yawn. "Is that my dog barking?"

G. W. Carver hopes it is more than her dog barking. He wishes his associates have finally come to rescue him.

"Maybe we're being robbed!" she squeals while jumping to her feet.

"No worries," G. W. Carver assures. "It's likely my associates coming to rescue me."

This news terrifies her even more. "More aliens in my home?" she gasps.

Downstairs, Cally looks back towards the yard and discovers she is all alone. Without warning a growling presence leaps out of the darkness and latches onto her ankle. It is Peppy, Kashonda's big black Rottweiler. Peppy tears deep into Cally's flesh, forcing her body to transmute into a menacing creature as well. Suddenly, the black panther appears and frightens Peppy into releasing his grip. He escapes from her grip down the hall and out of sight.

"Who is it!" screams Matilda after Peppy takes refuge under her bed. Matilda sleeps in the main floor suite near the kitchen. And since she is Peppy's designated feeder, he clings to her more than anyone else. Matilda grabs the baseball bat always kept behind her bedroom door and charges into the hallway. Right then the back door slams shut. "Are you alright baby?" she yells up the stairs to Kashonda.

"We're fine Grandma," she responds.

"We..?" Matilda questions. "Who's up there with you?"

"Oops!" she whispers. "Nobody Grandma," she assures her worried grandmother. "I'm on my way down…okay?"

While Kashonda makes her way downstairs, Cally changes back into human form and finds a place to hide in the backyard.

Kashonda is surprised to see her Grandmother guarding the back door with a baseball bat.

"Oh honey," Matilda cries. "If they would've hurt you, I don't know what I would've done."

"I'm fine Grandma," Kashonda tells her. She wraps a consoling arm around her trembling grandmother. Kashonda wonders whether her friend is correct in his assessment of the situation. Are his alien friends really out there?

"He scared Peppy. That's all," Matilda reassures them both. "It was just a prowler."

Matilda escorts the police inside her home to the scene of the crime. She tells them about the full-size Rottweiler cowering under her bed and the slamming of the back door.

"Judging from this blood on the floor," one officer says, "Your dog took a big piece out of this would-be burglar."

"Did you hear that honey?" Matilda asks while searching the room for Kashonda. Her granddaughter is not in the room. "Hmm," she notes. "I'm sure she'll be back in a moment."

Kashonda tip-toes back to her room to tell G. W. Carver all that has transpired so far.

"That's interesting," he says. "My fellow travelers are out there and I need you to carry me to them."

"Okay…Let's go," she exhales and changes out of her pajamas into a pair of jeans and oversized t-shirt.

He climbs down from the dresser and scurries towards the door until her foot abruptly blocks his path.

"I'll take you out there after the police leave and Grandmother goes back to bed. Deal?" she persuades.

"Yes. It's a deal," he agrees while assuring himself that the prowler really is part of his rescue team.

# CHAPTER 32

# REUNITED

Kashonda securely wraps G. W. Carver inside a silk scarf. Peppy begins sniffy around her the moment she sneaks downstairs into the mud room. He jumps up on her while wagging a stubby tail and sniffs at the wrapped bundle in her hand. He catches a whiff of G. W. Carver and begins barking out of control.

"Quiet!" she sternly commands while slipping him a treat. "Go to your bed!"

He chomps down hard on the dog biscuit and begs for more.

"Okay," she tells him. "One more is all you get." She tosses it across the room far away from the door, then, quickly slips out to the spacious backyard.

In the meantime, Cally is hiding in the thick of the bushes in the outer edge of the yard. She tears off part of her sleeve and uses it as a bandage for the wound on her leg. She keeps a watchful eye on the house while her senses alert her to G. W. Carver's location. Suddenly, a girl steps out of the back door and scans the yard. She bends down and unwraps something she's carrying in the palm of her hand. Cally can hardly keep still. It's G. W. Carver.

"I feel like I'm being watched," Kashonda shivers while wrapping her arms around her body.

"It's them!" G. W. Carver shouts. "Unwrap me now!" he orders.

She cautiously unrolls him onto the dew covered lawn. He tumbles, then, quickly scrambles back to his feet. And then, to Kashonda's surprise, he waves his arms through the air while shouting, "I'm here! Over here!"

"It's okay to come out now," he coaxes. "I know you're out here."

His pleads go unanswered. "I just knew they were coming for me tonight," he pouts.

"Don't give up yet, little man," Kashonda gently pats him on the head. "I'm sure they're out here somewhere."

Just as she gives him that word of encouragement, his keen ears hear rustling in the bushes.

Frank and Terry remain silent and dutifully wait for Cally to make the first move.

Cally senses the girl standing next to G. W. Carver can, indeed, be trusted. Just the same, she cautiously steps out from behind the bushes.

Kashonda can hardly believe her eyes. She never expected to see a woman, an African-American like herself, step out from behind the bushes.

"This is an alien?" she wonders aloud.

G. W. Carver clears his throat and glances Kashonda's way.

"Looks can be very deceiving," he cautions.

She was expecting a creature with two heads. And certainly something odd and unrecognizable, but, she didn't expect a woman.

Cally cagily steps across the lawn towards them and forces a generous smile she knew would put Kashonda at ease.

"Hi, my name is Cally!" Cally extends a hand for Kashonda to shake.

"Hold on here!" squawks G. W. Carver. "If there are to be any introductions, I will make them."

Kashonda drops Cally's hand and focuses her attention on her little friend. G. W. Carver surprises her by hoisting himself up onto the brick grill. Now that he is waist-level with everyone, he proudly makes the formal introductions.

"Kashonda, This is Cally," he introduces. "Now don't let her pleasant appearance fool you. I assure you, she's as alien as I am," he says while shaking an accusing finger at Cally. "Maybe she'll be human enough to explain to you why it took her 72 earth hours to locate the universe's most prestigious ambassador," he huffs. His weary hands intentionally rests on his hips.

"You're all right? I've been so worried," she tells him. "Get inside my backpack."

He snuggles down next to the tissues and rest inside of his makeshift home.

Cally positions herself directly in front of Kashonda. "Well— now that you know our secret what do you intend to do about it?"

"I've been sworn to secrecy," Kashonda quickly responds. "I promise, I'll never tell a soul," she swears.

She's bound to tell someone, Cally reasons. How can a child keep such a secret?

"Like a breath mint?" Cally offers. "No thanks," Kashonda waves the mint away.

"I insist," Cally pushes the mint into Kashonda's hand and she pops it into her mouth. After a few seconds the flavor becomes cooler and more pleasurable than any mint she has ever tasted. Every moment of pleasure she has previously experienced during her lifetime suddenly comes to mind. She feels every sensation and relives every fun event. She feels Tommy tickling her again in first grade. She experiences the joy of winning the 6th grade spelling bee. She feels the blushing love of John, her first crush in 4th grade. And remembers the joy of her first real birthday party at four years old. Kashonda laughs herself to tears with a laugh so loud and deep it undoubtedly is swelling up from the soul. Her grandmother and neighbors come outside while wondering what all the commotion is about. Matilda grabs hold of her in an attempt to shake her out of the seemingly drunken stupor she's in.

"Honey, are you all right? What's going on out here?" Matilda asks while leading her granddaughter back into the house.

Kashonda stumbles over the threshold. Her apparent confusion stuns Matilda as well as her mother who just enters the kitchen.

"We'd better get you into the house girl." Her mother slips an arm around her daughter's waist. "You're seeing a doctor first thing in the morning."

Terry jumps down from the tree. Frank follows suit and races to catch up with Cally. All of a sudden, Frank burps and spits up a couple of feathers at Cally's feet.

"No wonder you two were so quiet in those trees," she chuckles.

THE END

# EPILOGUE

The adventures of Tom Clancey and his alien friends continue in the sequel of "Rescue in Time" part 2. G. W. Carver is back with his associates and hesitant to record their blunders, but he does it anyway. In a hapless turn of events, another alien is whisked away by the Colorado River rapids. One of the Lazaradactile's goes missing and is found washed up on a beach. When the FBI get involved, the secret gets out. Cally, the shape-shifter, panics and decides to call an end to the mission. Get your copy of the "Rescue in Time", part 2 where amazing adventures, romance, and comedy continues.